The No-No Boys
忠義

Also by Teresa R. Funke

For adults:

Dancing in Combat Boots
and Other Stories of American Women
in World War II

Remember Wake

For younger readers:

The Home-Front Heroes Series

Doing My Part

Visit www.teresafunke.com to:

- Add your stories or your family's stories about the past.
- See pictures and read more about the real Home-Front Heroes.
- Learn more about the Japanese internment camps of WWII.
- Find out how to schedule Teresa to speak at your school or visit via webcast.

The No-No Boys

To the Lundeens!

Teresa Funke

So it never happens again.

Teresa R. Funke

This is a work of fiction. Names, places and some incidents have been changed.

Published by:

Victory House Press
3836 Tradition Drive
Fort Collins, Colorado 80526
www.victoryhousepress.com

Library of Congress Control Number 2009936551

Printed in Canada

ISBN 978-1-935571-11-7
(Previously published by Bailiwick Press, ISBN 978-1-934649-03-9)

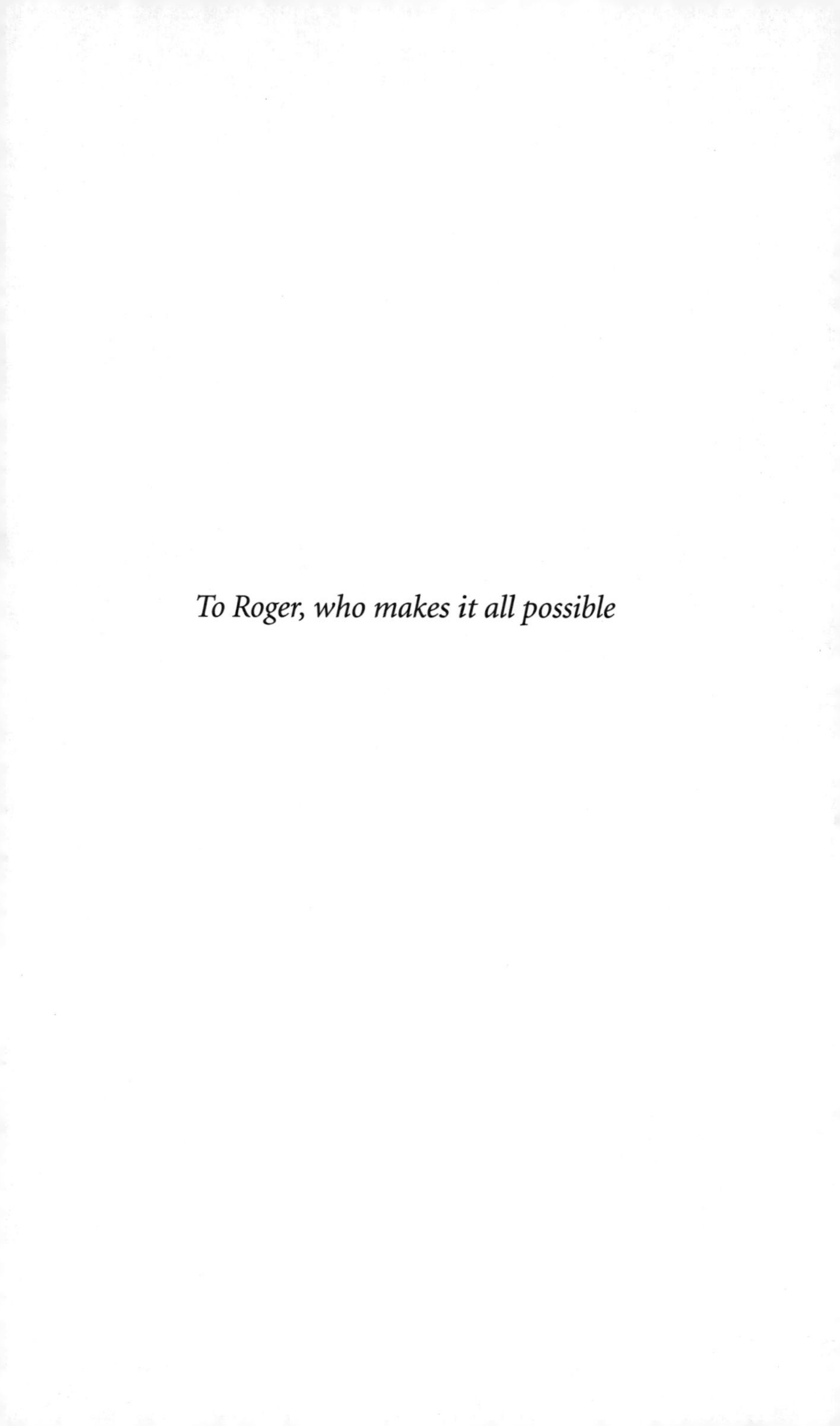

To Roger, who makes it all possible

Author's Note

What if you woke up one morning and were told that you and your family had three days to pack a few clothes and get ready to move to an unknown place? What if you had to sell or leave behind all your games, books, toys, even your pets? And then what if you ended up with thousands of other people living in a dusty, desolate camp surrounded by barbed wire and guard towers?

This actually happened to more than 55,000 Japanese-American children during World War II. It happened for a number of reasons, but mostly because people were scared. On December 7, 1941, the Japanese Imperial Navy attacked our U.S. Navy base at Pearl Harbor in Hawaii. The next day, America declared war on Japan, and later on Japan's ally, Germany. For Americans, this was the start of World War II. Americans were afraid that the Japanese people who lived here would try to help Japan take over America. It seems ridiculous now, of course, but people sometimes think ridiculous things in times of war.

Only two months after Pearl Harbor, in February, 1942, President Franklin D. Roosevelt issued Executive Order 9066, which said that all people of Japanese ancestry living on the West Coast of the United States had to be sent to relocation camps in California, Idaho, Utah, Colorado, Arizona, and Arkansas. Most of the kids who went to the camps were American citizens, born and raised right here in our country. They thought of themselves as regular American kids, just like their "Caucasian" friends.

With just a few days notice, Japanese-American families had to sell or give away nearly everything they owned and report for evacuation to the camps. They could bring with them only as much as each person could carry in suitcases or duffel bags. When they showed up to the train and bus stations, they had no idea where they were going.

My story takes place in Tule Lake Relocation Center in California during a difficult time in 1943. Most of the Japanese-Americans who were moved to the camps took pride in being law-abiding citizens, and despite the hardships of camp life, they tried to keep their spirits up. Their story has always inspired me. But when I started researching the camps, I discovered that a few of the Japanese-Americans were angry about being locked up. They caused trouble, especially at Tule Lake, and I wondered if I could really blame them. I might have been angry too.

I believe we study the past so we can learn from our mistakes and never repeat them. "I was a prisoner in my own country for three and a half years, and I'd done nothing wrong," Masaru Yamasaki told me. Mas was a teenager when he was sent to the camps. He now speaks to schoolchildren about his experience. "I tell my story because I hope something like this never happens in our country again."

It's up to us to make sure it doesn't.

1

Our Own Little City

忠義

"Go long, Tai!" Buck yells, and I dash off down the middle of the road, glancing back over my shoulder to watch the arc of the football. I pivot on my right foot and turn for the catch. Out of the corner of my eye, I see Kiomi watching. She's wearing a knee-length, wool coat and hugging her books to help fend off the cold. Her black hair lifts slightly in the February wind. I turn back just as the ball hits me in the chest and pull my hands up quick to catch it tight against me. It almost looks as if I had the whole thing planned.

"Yeah!" Buck whoops. He runs toward me, snatching at my coat sleeve as he loses his balance. The light February snow is melting, and the streets of camp have turned to a heavy mud that sucks at your shoes. Buck nearly takes us both down as my coat slides off my shoulder. We wrestle to stay upright. Neither of our mothers will be happy if we come home covered in mud.

I notice Kiomi giggling at us. "Get off," I tell Buck as I shove him back a bit and straighten my coat.

Buck takes the football from me and jerks his head toward the open fire break area near our high school. "Let's see if we can get a game going."

"Nah, I have to work. Besides, the ground's too slick. Didn't you just learn that lesson?"

Buck shrugs. A mischievous smile crosses his lips, and I know something is up.

"What?" I say, too late. I feel my collar come away from my neck and something icy cold slide down my back. Shigeru Tanaka has stuffed a handful of snow inside my coat. He's laughing and backing up to avoid my swing. Buck slaps me hard on the back, rubbing the snow into my skin.

"Ah, that's cold," I say, but even I'm laughing now as I reach for Shig. He has no difficulty dodging out of my way. He's always been faster than me—in foot races and judo anyway, but not in basketball. I've got him there. We've been like this since we were little boys, competitive, but he's one of my best friends. Him and Buck. We were all born in Sacramento, the capital of California, in a neighborhood called Japantown. We played together long before we came here to Tule Lake Relocation Center. Only we didn't have snow to play in then.

"Give me the ball," Shig says, and Buck tosses him the pigskin, but I knock it out of Shig's hands and catch it as it falls. Then I take off toward the back of the school. I hear Kiomi yell, "Run, Tai," and I do the best I can in the mud and snow.

When I'm back around the long barracks building that makes up part of the high school, I stop to wait for my friends. I'm still laughing a little, until I glimpse my older brother, Ben, walking by with two of the troublemakers he's been palling around with lately. He doesn't notice me at first. He's busy talking to the leader, Sonny, who wears aviator sunglasses even though it's cloudy today. Ben finally catches my eye. He gives me a slight nod, but that's it. He's walking in the direction of the newspaper, where my father works.

"Was that your brother?" Shig asks, coming up beside me.

"Uh-huh."

"He's with Sonny now, huh?"

"What about it?"

"Nothin'. My cousin's with him too," Shig says, and I see on his face a hint of worry. It's what I've been feeling lately too.

"Come on," Buck says. "Give me the ball." I smile at Shig and toss the football high in the air. We laugh as Buck scrambles to catch it.

"So what do you think?" Shig asks, leaning carefully against the tarpaper wall of the school to tie the laces of his work boot. "Should we try out for the football team next year?"

"Nah, I'll stick to basketball," I say. "And judo."

"There's gonna be a tournament, did you hear?" Shig says.

I straighten up. "A judo tournament? When?"

"Well, you'd know if you had come to the lesson last week. Sensei said it'll probably be this summer. We'll compete in the 13 and older division. I should say *you'll* compete. *I'll* win."

"When pigs fly." I give him a shove. "What about you, Buck? You gonna compete?"

"Nah, I'm no athlete. I'm the brains of this operation," he says, and I groan. If it weren't for my stopping by each night to help Buck with his homework, he'd likely never turn in a single assignment. School holds no interest for him. He's good with numbers, though. He learned those helping his father take bets on the sporting matches in camp. "No," he says, throwing his arm around my shoulder. "I'll just sit in the crowd and watch the match. Yep, me and pretty Kiomi cheering you on. *Gambatte!*"

I duck out from under his arm and move off before the guys can see my blush. "Hey, where ya goin'?" Buck calls. "I was only kiddin'."

"I gotta get to work. I'm late." I wave as I dash back around to the front of the school. Kiomi and her friends are gone, and Miss McAllister, my history teacher, is coming out the front door. "Tai," she calls. "Don't forget your report tomorrow. And remember to speak up when you deliver it to the class."

"I will, Miss McAllister," I say, and I can't get away from her fast enough. Teachers never seem to realize that when school's over, it's over. You're not supposed to bug the kids once they've left. It's bad enough spending half the day crowded around a long table with a bunch of other ninth graders listening to some boring lecture on the Civil War. When a guy's gone, he should be gone.

Once I'm out of earshot of my teacher, I switch to a walk. I should probably keep running. Papa doesn't like it when I'm late getting to the newspaper, but the wind has died down and it's warmed up a bit and it feels good to be alone for a few minutes. It's not easy finding time alone in camp. Not with 16,000 other bored people milling around. We're our own little city here at Tule Lake. Well, not a real city. Not like Sacramento with its movie houses and restaurants and tall, fancy buildings.

Back in Sacramento, my parents had owned a tofu shop, and we lived upstairs, in the rooms above. We didn't have much before the war—the Depression hit us hard—but we had our own radio for listening to shows like my favorite, *The Shadow*, and our own bathroom instead of a shared one like my cousins had, and I even had my own bike. Things were okay until the war came along.

When I was growing up, I never really thought of myself as Japanese. I was just a regular American kid. But a year ago, on December 7, I was coming home from playing basketball with my friends, and the neighbor boy ran up to me in the street. "Did you hear?" he said. "The Japs attacked Pearl Harbor."

"Where's that?" I asked.

"In Hawaii. They bombed our ships and planes at the naval base. They say we're going to war."

In that moment, I looked around and saw all of us living together in Japantown, speaking Japanese and eating rice and standing out in every way, and I wondered what was going to happen to us.

I didn't have to wait long to find out. Only two months later, President Roosevelt ordered us to leave our homes and move into these camps. It didn't matter if we were American citizens or not. Suddenly we were the enemy, no different from the ugly, buck-toothed Jap soldiers they draw in American newspaper cartoons. The government gave us only a few days to take care of our homes and businesses. Some of our neighbors had friends outside of Japantown who could keep some of their stuff. Others had enough money to rent a storage unit. But my family had neither of those. So we gave away some of our belongings and sold the rest for much less than they were worth. Anything that looked Japanese we had burned right after Pearl Harbor, including my old judo uniform and Mama's wedding *kimono*. We had been renting the space for the store and our apartment, so we had no home to lose, but we did have the tofu machines and other equipment we'd bought. We simply locked up the shop and left it all behind. Then we reported for evacuation, bringing with us only what we could carry.

First the government took us to an assembly

center, which was really a camp they'd thrown together at a racetrack. Our barracks were old horse stalls, and they stank of manure. We stayed there for several weeks, until Tule Lake was ready for us. We got here on a hot, dusty day last summer.

We've been in Tule Lake seven months, and we're used to it now. But sometimes I think about our little apartment in Japantown, and I miss our radio and my bike, but I especially miss my baseball card collection. I wanted to bring it with me, but Mama said no toys. She'd sewn us duffel bags, and she wanted as much room as possible for packing clothes, not knowing what the weather would be like here in northern California. So I gave my cards to a Caucasian kid at school. She was right, I guess, but not a day goes by that I don't kick myself for not bringing at least my Babe Ruth and Lou Gehrig cards, my two favorite players.

I jam my hands deep in my pockets and hunch into the cold as I leave Block 71. Tule Lake is made up of blocks, but instead of houses and stores and businesses in each block, we have fourteen long, wooden barracks buildings. In each building, several families live in their own tiny apartments. Each block also has a mess hall, a recreation hall, a laundry room, and men's and women's latrines, where we shower together. If you stand in Block 24 in the center of camp, where my family lives, all you can see far off into the distance is row after row of barracks.

Like I said, we're our own little city. We call ourselves Tuleans, and we try to consider this place home, at least for now, but every one of us thinks about life outside. Our mothers long to fix Japanese food again in their own kitchens, instead of lining up for army chow in the mess halls. Our fathers pine away for the respect they once had in their former jobs. Our older sisters daydream about the places their boyfriends will take them when there is more to do than the occasional dance in camp. Our older brothers boast about the cars they're going to buy when we get out. And me? I daydream about playing basketball on a real indoor court again, not some uneven, pockmarked patch of dirt.

But mostly I think about how my family was before Tule Lake, how we used to get along. This place has changed my brother, Ben, and I'd gladly do without the things I left behind if I could just get my fun-loving brother back. But I can hear as I approach the newspaper office that the old Ben is still missing. The new Ben, this angry, frustrated Ben I hardly recognize, is doing something he never would have done before. He's yelling at my father.

2
A Question of Loyalty
忠義

I wait outside the *Daily Tulean Dispatch* office for a few minutes, listening through the cracked-open door to my father and brother argue. I'm guessing none of the other employees are in the room, or Papa would never allow such a scene to take place. Even still, the walls in the barracks are so thin, people in the rooms next to the newspaper can surely hear every word my brother is saying. There are no secrets at Tule Lake.

I push the door open quietly and take a tentative step inside the wide room. I see Ben and my father standing in a corner, Ben resembling Papa more and more each day, with the same round-rimmed glasses, long, thin build and sharp shoulders. I take after my mother, shorter and stockier than Ben, with my mother's round face. Ben's arms are folded tight across his chest, his back rounded like he's holding in his rage, his eyes defiant. Papa is standing straight, his right hand raised, palm turned toward Ben as if he's trying to get him to understand. They are arguing about the War Relocation Authority's new loyalty questionnaire. It's the same argument they've been having for days. In fact, everyone in camp is arguing about it. At fourteen, I'm not old enough to sign it, but I know exactly what's upsetting everyone. It's Question 27 and Question 28. Question 27 asks if the person signing is willing to serve in the U.S. Army, and Question 28 asks if you will swear allegiance only to the United States and give up loyalty to any other country. In our case, that means Japan.

"You must sign 'yes' to the questions on the questionnaire, Ben," Papa is saying in Japanese. "You must show the government you are true to America."

I can almost guess what Ben will say next.

"Why should I?" he answers in English. Though our parents speak mostly Japanese, they can understand a little English, and though Ben and I speak mostly English, we can understand most Japanese. It's like this for nearly all my friends. We are both American and Japanese, but lately Ben has been feeling more Japanese than American. "Why should I show my loyalty to a country that has locked me up like a prisoner?" Ben demands.

"This is not a prison, Ben," Papa says, lowering his hand.

"Look around you, Papa. Can't you see the barbed wire fence that keeps us in and the guards in the towers with their machine guns pointing at us? Are we allowed to go home to Sacramento? Are we allowed to even leave the camp without permission? If this is not a prison, what would you call it?"

As I try to remove my coat, my weight shifts and the floorboard creaks. Papa notices me for the first time. It's me he looks at when he answers Ben. "I know it feels like a prison sometimes," Papa says. "Maybe especially to a young man who's anxious to make his way in the world. But this is where our life is now, at least until the war's over. *Shikata ga nai*, son. It can't be helped. It must be endured."

Ben throws up his hands. "You're hopeless, you with your old-fashioned attitudes. What good is it to hold onto Japanese ideals in a place like this? The Caucasians don't see any honor in our cooperation. Some of them are even saying that our quiet behavior, our willingness to accept this with no complaint, simply proves we are up to something. No matter what we do, we can't win with these people, yet you want me to swear allegiance to them? To say

I'm willing to fight in their army and die, while they keep my family locked away. I won't do it, Papa. I'm eighteen. The decision is mine, not yours."

I hear myself gasp, and Ben turns to look at me. In a Japanese family, you respect your parents above all else, and my reaction seems to remind Ben how wrong he is to talk back to our father. He lowers his head, but his fists are still clenched. "I'll see you tonight after dinner," he mumbles and quickly leaves.

For a long moment, Papa stands rooted in place, his eyes staring past the spot where Ben just stood and out the paned-glass window. I could say something, but I know this expression on Papa's face. He's going inside himself. He's pulling his feelings back in. When's he's ready, he'll speak to me, tell me which jobs he wants me to start on first. I fold my coat and lay it over the bench by one of the rough picnic tables that hold our equipment and typewriters, our stacks of paper and old issues of the newspaper. It feels cool in the room, and I check the potbelly stove. The coal is low, so I scoop in a new shovelful and close the door.

Papa moves past me to gather up some ink bottles and put them back in their place. When he first came to America, he worked on the San

Francisco docks like many other Japanese men. When he'd made enough money, he moved to Sacramento and got a job as a typesetter at the Japanese newspaper then worked his way up to reporter. When Ben was born, he wanted to make more money, so he opened the tofu store. Tofu is pressed bean curd, and it's used a lot in Japanese cooking, so Papa thought his store would do well. But then the Depression came, and even though Papa worked very hard, we never did make much money. Things were just starting to get better for us when the war started. Since he can't own a tofu store in camp, he's working at the barber shop. He smells like shampoo and hair tonic. I think he misses having his own business, but he never complains. Whenever he can, he knocks off work early to help at the newspaper. He's like that. He believes in helping wherever he can. He thinks my brother and I should be that way too. That's why I have to help at the newspaper whenever Papa's working there. Most of the paper is written in English, but Papa writes a few articles in Japanese for his fellow *Issei*, people who moved here from Japan and don't speak much English.

He turns and smiles at me now, but his eyes

appear tired behind his glasses. "How was school today?" he asks in Japanese.

"Fine," I say. "Same old thing."

"If it is the same old thing, then you are the same old thing," Papa says. "Every day there is something new to learn. Education is important, son."

I roll my eyes. "I know, Papa."

"Then tell me something you learned today that was not the same old thing."

I sigh. He does this all the time, makes me tell him what I've learned. I used to think he did it so he could learn new things himself, but now I'm not so sure. I think he understands more about America than he lets on.

"I learned that Abraham Lincoln freed the slaves."

"And how did he free them?"

"With a document called the Emancipation Proclamation."

"You see what an amazing country this is, Taichirou? With only a piece of paper and a man's word, a whole group of people found their freedom."

"It was only a piece of paper and a man's word that took our freedom away," I mutter under my breath. I'm speaking of President Roosevelt's Executive Order 9066, which sent us to these camps.

I'm still thinking about Papa's argument with Ben and wondering if Ben might be right. If maybe we should be a little more angry about how we've been treated. But I don't want to upset Papa again, so I change the subject.

"Papa, I forgot to tell you! There's going to be a judo tournament this summer. Shig thinks he can win it, but I think I can beat him if you and Ben work with me on my moves. Will you help me?"

Papa nods as he stacks mimeograph paper on a shelf. "A judo tournament is a good thing. I competed myself in many tournaments when I was a boy in Japan."

"I know, Papa."

"You must listen to your Sensei. Pay attention to your training, learn the *reigi* and you will do well."

"I know, Papa."

"With judo you can protect yourself and your family, but it also teaches you respect and —"

"Loyalty," I interrupt. I know this lecture by heart.

He turns to me and smiles. "Yes, loyalty. A tournament gives you a chance to do your best, Tai. If you can achieve your best in all you do, our whole society benefits. This is what I was taught when I was in Japan. This is what you must learn here."

"I will, Papa."

"Good. Enough talk then. You have work to do. The light on the light table keeps going on and off. You fix it."

He's giving me this job because I'm good with mechanical things. Back home, whenever the tofu machine quit working, I was the only one who could get it running again. I reach under the table and jiggle the light bulb.

"The wire behind the socket is loose," I say.

"Uh?"

He doesn't understand the English word "socket," and I don't know how to say it in Japanese. "I need some electrical tape." He shakes his head, so I mimic the motion of taping a wire.

"Ah, ah," he says. "Nothing like that here."

I survey the room until I spot a ball of string. That will work for the moment. I tie up the loose wire to the one next to it, and the light comes on.

"You got it working!" one of the reporters says as he comes into the room. His name is Tom, and he's assigned to cover sports in our camp. Even with his winter clothes on, you can tell by his build he's a pretty good athlete himself. That's one of the reasons the girls like him so much. I don't pay much attention to most of the stories when I'm helping print off the newspaper, but I *always* read the sports page. Now that football season is over, Tom can start reporting on other sports in more detail. He's friendly to me—like Ben used to be—and I tell him in a few months he'll be writing about me and the judo tournament.

"Oh I don't know anything about judo," he says. "Our farm was too far out for me to participate in many Japanese things."

Tom is not from California. He's from eastern Washington, from a small town with only a few Japanese. "What did you grow on your farm, Tom?"

"*We* didn't grow anything. We worked for a farmer who grew strawberries. It was always my father's plan that when I got old enough, I'd buy us some land and we'd start our own farm. Since Papa's from Japan, he's not allowed to own land, you know? He saved up money for years for that dream, but now that I'm finally old enough, we're here. And who knows how long the war will last." He doesn't sound mad when he says it—not like Ben would; he just sounds disappointed.

"Don't you think it's unfair that your father

can't own land?" I say. "Ben says our parents should be angry about that. And he says they should be angry that the government has never allowed them to become citizens just because they were born in Japan."

"Is that right?" Tom is only a year or two older than Ben, but sometimes he seems much older. "I guess Ben's got a point. But my father never saw it that way. He was just glad that I was a U.S. citizen and could own land. It's a way for our family to move ahead in this country. I'm sure your father feels the same way."

I glance over at my dad. He's inking the mimeograph machine and paying no attention to our English conversation.

"Hey, Tom. If you want, I can teach you a little about judo. Then you can write about it in the paper. I'm going to win the tournament, you know?" I say, puffing out my chest in a mocking way.

Tom squeezes my shoulder. "Yeah, you just might, kid. We'll talk about it later, okay? Right now I gotta hoof it over to the mess hall. I'm covering my brother's shift. He's got that cold that's going around camp. Course, he's not as sick as he's making out to be. He's just lazy. But he's got Mama fooled. See ya later, Tai."

Tom waves at my father as he jumps out the door. I watch him pull his collar up high around his ears as he leans into the wind and hurries off. I wish I could get Ben to pal around with Tom instead of those hotheads he's been hanging out with lately. Until he started eating dinner with them in the mess hall every night instead of our family, he seemed okay. Now we hardly see him, except when he comes home to sleep. A couple of weeks ago, he lost his job at the motor pool because his boss didn't want to listen to his anti-American talk anymore. And now all the good jobs are taken, so Ben's stuck cleaning the latrines. Maybe that's another reason he's been so out of sorts lately. I would be too if I had to swab toilets. But as Shig would say, that's his own doing. I just wish there was some way I could help.

Maybe I'll talk to Ben tonight about the judo tournament. He used to be pretty good at judo. Maybe I could get him to compete, too, or at least to help me. It'd be like it used to be back home when we'd practice our moves together before bed, sometimes getting so wound up we'd knock into the furniture, and Mama would scold us from the other side of the bedroom door. Yeah, that's what I'll do. I'll talk to Ben. We'll do the judo tournament together. We've got months to practice. It'll be great.

3

Eiko's Gift

忠義

Papa and I leave the *Dispatch* office together. It's getting colder, and the ground is hardening as it starts to freeze. We meet Mama halfway to the mess hall. The three of us stand in line for runny mashed potatoes, stewed corn, and a spot of tough beef. Mama groans as the attendants ladle the food onto her plate. She liked to cook before the war, but American food doesn't agree with her stomach. I see Shig and Buck and some of the other guys from our block eating together at a table.

"I'm gonna eat with the guys," I tell Mama.

"Uh-uh. You eat with us tonight. When we're finished, we will go visit Eiko. Her baby will be here soon."

Eiko is my cousin. "Can't you just call me when you're ready to leave?"

"Tai," Papa's voice is firm. "Do as your mother says."

I follow my parents to a long table and sit down, glancing wistfully at my friends. They're laughing, while my family eats in silence. But I'm excited too about visiting my cousin. In Japantown, Eiko's family lived only a few apartments down from mine. I saw her nearly every day. When I was a kid, she used to make me rice cakes and talk baseball with me. She's a real baseball nut, which is odd for a girl. In fact, many of the cards in my collection came from Eiko. But Eiko married her boyfriend, Dan Hirata, a few months before the war started, and now they live in Block 12, which is two blocks away, so I don't see her as much anymore. But we're all excited about the baby. It'll be the first new baby in our family since I was born.

I take one last look around for Ben before we leave the mess hall, but Papa tugs at my sleeve. He points at Mama, indicating that I should carry the carefully wrapped bundle of baby blankets and clothes she has sewn. Even without her sewing machine, Mama is an excellent seamstress. When we first arrived at camp, there was nothing in our twenty foot by twenty foot room except four steel army cots and mattresses we had to stuff with straw. Papa took one of the scratchy, wool blankets we'd been given and hung it as a divider, with him and Mama on one side and Ben and I on the other.

For the first three nights, I could hear Mama crying when she thought I was asleep, but by the fourth day, she had collected herself. She sent Papa off with Buck's dad to scavenge scrap lumber left over from when they built the camp. Buck's dad made us a rough-hewn table and two benches. Over time, Ben and I added shelves to the walls, and we were so proud of ourselves when we surprised Mama on her birthday with a tall wardrobe with a door to help keep the dust off her clothes.

Now, all these months later, Mama has transformed our drab, drafty room into something closer to home. There are curtains on the windows and a tablecloth on the table, and the shelves are covered with seashell decorations she's made. Tule Lake is built on a dry lake bed, and seashells are almost as common as pebbles in the dirt around camp. The trick is finding the ones that aren't broken.

We reach Eiko's apartment just as my fingers are turning numb. Eiko answers the door and bows to my parents. She and Mama move off toward the center of the room, where Eiko shows off the baby clothes and blankets to her mother-in-law, Mrs. Hirata. Mrs. Hirata praises my mother's stitches, and Mama covers her mouth, embarrassed, but I can tell she's also pleased. Papa and I remove our coats, and Eiko's husband, Dan, lays them over a bench by the door. Mr. Hirata asks Papa if he'd like to play *hana*, a Japanese card game. Dan moves over to join them. None of them address me, so I'm not sure if I should ask to play or not. Just then Eiko comes up beside me and touches my elbow. "Come here," she says. "I have something for you."

I follow her behind the blanket partition that hides Eiko's and Dan's bed and a used bassinet that's all set up for the baby. Eiko takes my arms and sits me down on the bed. She's got that playful look on her face, the one that makes her black eyes shine and her cheeks flush. She removes her coat from a nail on the wall, revealing her handbag hanging beneath it and struggles with the clasp on her bag, which is sticking shut. She wrinkles up her nose at me, which is about the only hint of frustration Eiko ever shows. When the clasp finally pops open, she rummages inside and pulls something out. She hides her hand behind her back, which makes her big belly stick out even further. She's grinning broadly.

"What is it?" I ask.

"Guess."

"I don't know."

"Just guess."

I groan. "A stick of gum."

"Nope."

"An extra ration stamp."

"Nope."

"I give up."

She pulls out her hand and proudly turns her palm over. Lying there is a Lou Gehrig baseball card just like the one I left behind. I snatch it from her.

"Where'd you get this?"

"A man came into the store the other day to buy a new sweater. We started talking about baseball, and he told me about his collection of cards. He's a bachelor, so he had plenty of room in his two suitcases to bring a few personal belongings to the camp, including his collection. I asked him if he'd sell me a card or two, and he said the only extra one he had was a Lou Gehrig. Can you believe it, Tai?"

I shake my head, beaming at the card. It's almost as good as having my whole collection back. Then I think about what Eiko said. I know she won't be able to work at the store once the baby arrives, which means they'll have to get by on Dan's income as a baker. "How much did this cost you, Eiko?"

"Never you mind. It's a gift. Don't you know you're not supposed to ask the price of a gift?"

"I can pay you back," I offer. "Papa gives me a little money for helping out at the paper."

"I heard. What have you been spending your money on?"

"Candy mostly, when they're not out at the canteen. And I give some of it to Mama. But I have enough to pay you back."

She lays her hand on my shoulder. "I don't want your money, Tai. I just wanted you to have something special. I used to give you a baseball card every year on your birthday, remember? But this past birthday we were all here. So consider this a late birthday present."

I want to hug her, but I'm getting too old for that. Instead I offer to fix the clasp on her purse. "Do you have any hair oil?"

"Dan has some." She takes a tube of Brylcreem off the shelf.

I squeeze some of the greasy cream onto my finger and use it to oil the stuck clasp. "So what do you think the baby is, Eiko? A boy or a girl?"

"I don't know. My mother-in-law is sure it's a boy, but I think it's a girl. What do you think?"

I shrug. "I'll come and see you in the hospital when it's born."

"I'd like that, Tai."

Just then my mother calls for us. I tuck the card into the back pocket of my jeans and duck back around the curtain. Eiko's mother-in-law has made real green tea in a kettle on an electric hot plate. My mother is thrilled. The Hiratas have friends in Klamath Falls, Oregon, which is only thirty-five miles away. They come to the camp every few weeks to bring items Mrs. Hirata has requested from the outside. We know the tea must be special to them, and they probably don't have much of it, so this is an honor. Papa and Dan and Mr. Hirata stop their card game and pull the benches up to the table, where we hold the cups in our hands and sip appreciatively.

"Where is your other son?" Mr. Hirata asks.

I glance at Eiko. Papa glances at Mama. "He couldn't make it tonight," Papa says.

"These young people have lost their respect for family," Mr. Hirata adds. "They run wild in the camp. There is no discipline here."

Papa nods politely. "It's a difficult time for young

men. The new loyalty oath has them confused."

"Not so confusing," Mr. Hirata says. "We must obey the government. We must show our loyalty."

The only part of Papa's body that stirs is the index finger of his right hand, which taps lightly on the table. "Yes, but to sign yes to the questions on the loyalty oath means you must be willing to join the army if you are called. How does my son know what kind of treatment he will get in the army?"

"It does not matter the treatment. A soldier must fight with honor."

"And must a soldier die for a country that has treated him with disrespect?"

"A soldier must fight no matter what."

My father shifts in his seat. "My son is a man of honor. He will not disgrace his family, but he needs more time."

"Is it a disgrace to follow what you believe in, Papa?" I hear myself ask. My mother makes a shushing sound, and I lower my head.

Papa folds his hands on the table and says nothing. Mr. Hirata also says nothing. We let the moment pass, and then my mother and the other women clear the table. Dan gathers our coats. My parents bow low to Eiko's in-laws and thank them for their hospitality. Eiko pulls me aside and says, "Bring Ben with you when you come to the hospital. I haven't seen him in so long." I promise her I will, and she walks me to the door. She stands in the doorway and waves to us as we leave. I take the baseball card from my pocket and hold it up to her, and she smiles.

"What's that?" Mama asks.

"Nothing. Just a gift from Eiko."

Papa is still silent.

"I'm sorry I spoke up," I say to him.

"You were going to say more, Taichirou. What was it?"

"I don't know, Papa. Just that maybe Ben is right. Plenty of people in Tule Lake aren't signing yes on the questionnaire. Some of them are even talking about moving back to Japan."

Papa stops dead and faces me with a scowl. Mama steps back to give us room. "There is nothing for us in Japan," he says, his voice rising. "I was the youngest son of a youngest son. There was nothing for me to inherit, no future. I came to America to find work, and I found it. When I had enough money, I went to the *baishakunin*, the matchmaker, to help me arrange a picture marriage. She showed me many pictures, but when I saw the photograph of your mother, I knew she was the one. Her parents were dead. She was living with an old aunt. She had nothing either, until she came to America to marry me. Japan is our homeland, but this is our country now. This is *your* country, Taichirou. And your brother's. You must honor it."

"I will, Papa." The night is bitter cold, but my cheeks are hot from my embarrassment. I hope my father will let us go home now, get off the street where people can see me being scolded like a little kid. Mama is shivering, and she quietly suggests we get in out of the cold. Papa sighs deeply and looks at me as if he doesn't know what to do with me. Then he turns and heads off toward our block. I glance at Mama, who nods for me to follow. I wonder if Ben is home. I want to tell him how Papa stuck up for him at Mr. Hirata's, but I also want to tell him that maybe he should listen to what Papa says. Maybe it would be better for all of us if he'd just sign yes on that stupid questionnaire. At least then we could stop talking about it and all get along again.

4

The Attack

忠義

Two nights later we are getting ready for bed. It's my job to make sure the potbelly stove is well stoked for the night. Even with the stove, we'll use all of our blankets tonight. The boards in the barracks walls don't fit tightly together. In the winter, the wind and cold snake through the cracks between the boards. In the summer, the dust and insects creep in the same way. We've stuffed paper in many of the holes and bought throw rugs at the camp store to cover the worst spots in the floor. We've even nailed scrap lumber over the biggest cracks and, of course, we stuff rags in the opening under the door, but still the cold seeps in. On the worst nights, we sleep with our coats on.

I'm reading *Oliver Twist* by the light of a small table lamp that sits on my suitcase, which serves as a table. I'm trying to shut out the sounds of the Yamamoto family, who live in the unit next door.

Since our walls don't go all the way to the ceiling, we can hear their conversations, their laughter, even their disagreements. It makes it hard to concentrate sometimes.

My mother pokes her head around the curtain. She's wearing her dressing gown with her coat over it, ready for bed.

"Reading?" she says.

"Yes."

"Good book?"

"It's okay." She's still standing there, so I continue. "Our English teacher said we have to read a Charles Dickens book. I wanted *A Tale of Two Cities*. It's set in the French Revolution and there's fighting and guillotines, but the Endo twins have been hogging it, so I got stuck with this one."

Mama laughs.

Just then we hear Ben at the front door. "Keep reading," Mama says, but I drop my book on my cot and push the curtain aside. Ben stomps the mud off his boots outside and leans in the doorway as he pulls them off and hands them to Mama, who sets them on a piece of newspaper on the floor. After Ben enters, he hands Mama his coat, then stuffs the rags in the crack beneath the door. Papa has been reading his own book in the scrap-wood chair by the stove. He closes the book and stands to face my brother.

"It's late," he says. "Where have you been?"

"Out."

"Where out?"

Ben is warming his hands at the stove, his back to Papa. "Out with friends."

"What were you doing with these friends?"

"Nothing, Papa. We were just talking."

I can tell by the set of his jaw that Papa wants to say more. He reaches up and scratches his scalp beneath his dark hair. There are streaks of grey at his temples that weren't there before the evacuation. He glances over at Mama. She shakes her head slightly. Papa gives a long, stern look at Ben and then stalks across the room and sits down hard on his cot, staring at his hands.

Ben relaxes his stance. He glances at me and does something unexpected. He winks. I feel my shoulders drop, and I smile at him. "Good-night," he mutters to my parents as he crosses the room and pushes the divider aside. I stand back to let him in. "I went to judo lesson tonight, Ben," I say eagerly. "I thought you might come."

"I had other things to do."

"We worked on *ne-waza* today. I'm getting better at it. The holds are harder for me, you know? I'm not as big as Shig and the other guys."

"Size has nothing to do with it," Ben says.

"I was sparring with Shig tonight. I held him for eighteen seconds. I need to get to twenty-five."

"Okay then. Show me your moves." Ben pushes his cot aside and drops to his knees for ground sparring.

I lower myself in front of him. We lock arms and grapple to pin each other down. It feels so good to be sparring with Ben again that I start to laugh.

"Be serious," he says, but he's smiling too. "If you're not serious, you can't win."

In the past, Ben would have taken only a minute to pin me, but I'm holding my own now, especially since I've stopped laughing and started concentrating. Ben's face changes. The smile departs, and his eyes go cold.

"You've gotten stronger," he says. "If this were a street fight, though, I'd have you. You've left yourself too open. All I'd have to do is punch you here, and you'd go down." He gives me a sharp jab in the side. I'm not hurt, just stunned. I drop my arms.

"Sensei says judo is for defense," I say. "Not

offense. It's not supposed to be used for fighting."

"That's only half true," Ben says, standing up and dusting off his pants. "In the old days, samurai warriors would pin an opponent so they could stab him or finish him off some other way."

I realize now my knees are aching from the wood floor, and I stand up slowly. I study my brother as he takes off his socks, which are caked in mud above the ankles, and changes them out with a new pair from his duffel bag. I shiver as the cold hits me, and I crawl into my bed, pulling up the covers. Ben reaches over and switches off the lamp, and the room goes dark. Our parents are already asleep. When Ben settles into his cot, it feels like it used to when we shared a room in the apartment in Japantown. Then again, it doesn't. Ben has definitely changed, and his change scares me. I'm still happy to have his attention right now, though, and I want to say something that will keep this moment going, but what? What would this new Ben want to hear?

"I think you'd make a good warrior," I say.

"What do you mean? In the army? I'll never join the army. Not this army."

"But if you did, you'd fight well, maybe even win a medal."

Ben is silent for a moment, and I wonder if he's thinking about that medal. Maybe he's never thought of that possibility before. It'd be something, wouldn't it, to win a medal? "Hmm," is all he says. I wait to hear if he'll say more, but he doesn't. I roll away from him, and then I hear him whisper.

"Little brother?" He hasn't called me this in weeks.

"What?" I say, leaning out of my cot so I can hear him.

"Come with me tomorrow night."

"Where?"

"To a meeting with my friends."

"What kind of meeting?"

"Just come."

I shiver, and I'm not sure if it's from the cold or this feeling I have that something's not right. But Ben is including me in something, and I'm curious. Curious to see what it is that has taken him away from us. "Okay," I say. Then I pull the covers up over my head for warmth and to shut out the chill of this bad feeling.

The next day, I'm eating dinner in the mess hall with Buck and Jimi and Shig, who's just shown up late. We're digging into our hot-dog-and-eggs casserole, a dish only the army could dream up. We call it Weenie Royale. Kiomi and some of her friends are sitting at the next table over, still wearing their majorette uniforms from practice and chattering about their routine for the talent show. Kiomi's the best baton twirler in the bunch, and I'm listening to make sure they give her the lead role. Then I notice that Kiomi's coat has slipped off the bench onto the floor.

"Um, your coat," I say, leaning across the aisle.

"My what?"

"Your coat. It's on the floor."

She twists around. "Oh, thank you, Tai." The other girls are studying me now. Two of them are whispering to each other. I turn away, but Kiomi says, "Are you going to be in the talent show, Tai?"

"Me? Nah."

"Why not?"

"He's got no talent," Buck says.

"No one's talking to you, Buck," one of Kiomi's friends says.

"Well, no one's talking to you either."

"Stop it you two." Kiomi shakes her head at me.

I give her a half-smile, but I wish she'd quit talking to me in front of my friends. Buck and Jimi are making lovesick eyes at each other and smooching noises. I'm glaring at them across the table when Shig saves me by sliding suddenly onto the bench beside me, putting some distance between me and Kiomi.

"Where you been?" I ask.

"At the administration building."

"Why?"

"My cousin Yoshi was there for a while. He was with a group of boys who beat up an *inu* this afternoon, but he wasn't the leader, so they let him go." An *inu* is what some people in camp call anyone who is helping the Caucasians. I wonder if Ben was with Yoshi, but I don't want to ask in front of the other guys, and I figure Shig would have said if he was.

"Who'd they get?" Buck asks. He sounds a little excited. "Who was the *inu*?"

"Mr. Sato."

"Mr. Sato?" I say. "I know him. He's not an *inu*. He used to teach English in our neighborhood. He helps people translate in the camp. He's even helped us translate some stories at the paper."

"Well, my cousin says he spies for the Caucasians. He says Mr. Sato takes what he hears and reports it back to the camp commander."

"But that's crazy," I say, dropping my fork. "Mr. Sato's just a quiet, old man."

"Take it easy, Tai. It's not like they killed him or nothin'. He's just in the hospital with a couple of broken ribs."

I glance around the table to see if this news bothers anyone but me, but the other guys have tucked back into their food. Ever since the trouble with the loyalty questionnaire began, the No-No Boys, as we now call them—the ones who have refused to sign yes to the two questions on the loyalty questionnaire—have started causing more problems. I know my mother's afraid Ben might be one of them, but Ben hasn't said if he is or not. All I can hope is that Ben wasn't a part of this. Not Mr. Sato. Ben knows him as well as I do. I glance over at Kiomi's table and find her watching me closely. Among her friends, only she seems to have noticed something is wrong. She smiles at me gently, but I look away. I ask Shig if he wants what's left of my food, and he takes it eagerly. I have to find my brother.

5

A Dangerous Request

忠義

I rush home, but Ben's not there. Mama's lying down, a couple of blankets tucked under her chin, her hand resting on her stomach. During the day, she's mostly fine, but often in the evening, she gets terrible stomachaches. She says it's the food, but Papa thinks it's the worry. I'm not even sure if she went to dinner tonight, but there's a cup of cold coffee on the floor by her cot. She asks where I'm going, and I say I'm heading over to Buck's to help him with homework. It's not entirely a lie. I probably will go there after I meet up with Ben. She asks me to bring her a blanket from my bed. As I cover her up, she seems small and frail. There are dark circles under her eyes, and her face looks drawn.

"You okay, Mama?" I ask.

"I'm fine. Just my stomach."

I pick up the cup and swirl the thin, black coffee. "Do you want this? I could heat it up on the hot plate."

"No, no. Put it on the table. Coffee's no good. What I need is some tea."

"I could go to Mrs. Hirata's to see if she could lend us some."

"No, Tai. I'll be fine. Your father will be home soon." She strokes my arm to reassure me. "You're so serious these days. You were not that way before evacuation. Always worrying now. Go to your friend's, son. I'll be all right."

I nod and pull my boots on by the door. I glance at Mama, but she waves me on. I look up and down the street, wondering where I can find Ben. I'm supposed to meet him at his friend Sonny's apartment at seven o'clock, but I want to talk to him before he's around his new gang. Ben doesn't bum around much with the guys he knew back in Sacramento. He wasn't as lucky as me. His best friends's families didn't come to Tule Lake the way mine did. They were sent to camps in Utah and Arizona. That's how he fell in with guys like Sonny. I've only met Sonny once or twice, but I don't like him. He's older than Ben, and he shows it off by bossing Ben around. He's got a look about him that's, I don't know, kind of mean. It wouldn't surprise me a bit to find out Sonny was the ringleader on the attack on Mr. Sato.

Since Ben wasn't in the mess hall and he wasn't at home, I've got no choice but to walk around till seven and then head over to Sonny's, unless I can head Ben off first. Yeah, that's what I'll do. I'll wait for him at the corner of Sonny's barracks and see if I can catch him before he goes in. I dash up to Block 30 and huddle next to the barracks with my back to the wind. My stomach growls. I should have finished my dinner. I've got a stash of candy hidden in my duffel bag back at our apartment. Maybe when we get home, I can share a Hershey's bar with Ben—that is, if he tells me he had nothing to do with Mr. Sato. If he tells me he was involved, I'm not sure what I'll do.

A few minutes before seven, I see Ben walking along. He's not alone. I should have known. Ben's never alone these days. But he's not with his friends either. He's with a girl. I don't recognize her, but she and Ben seem pretty familiar. She's tall for a Japanese, and unlike the other girls who wear pageboy hair styles, she wears her hair in one long braid down her back. Ben grips her coat with both hands and pulls her playfully toward him. For a minute I think he's going to kiss her, and then he notices me. He whispers something in her ear, and she glances in my direction. She gives me a tiny wave and turns back the way she came. Ben watches her for a second, then jogs over to me. He's got a goofy grin on his face, and for a minute I forget that I might be mad at him. As he comes closer, I reach out and shove him with one hand. "So who's the girl, Benny boy?"

He shoves me back. "No one you need to know."

"Ben's got a girlfriend."

"Ah grow up, little brother. Come on, let's go inside."

I grab his arm. "Hold up, Ben."

He looks down at my hand and then up at my face and his grin fades. "What's with you, little brother?"

"Did you hear about Mr. Sato?"

"Yeah, so?"'

"Were you part of it?"

"Who wants to know?"

"I do."

He backs me up against the barracks. "Mr. Sato had it comin', Tai. Stay out of it, okay?"

"So you helped?" I push him away from me.

"No, I didn't. I was at work scrubbing toilets,

remember?"

"But you would have helped?"

"I don't know. Maybe."

"But Ben—"

"And quit calling me Ben." His voice sounds menacing. "Call me Benjiro."

I frown. "But I've always called you Ben. Everybody has."

"Well, I don't go by that name anymore. It sounds too American. I use my Japanese name now. So should you."

"Why should I? I'm not like you, *Ben*. I'm happy with the way I am."

"That's 'cause you're young and stupid. You don't see what's goin' on right around you, Tai. You need to open your eyes. Come on inside and let Sonny and me explain it." He reaches for me, but I jerk away.

"I don't like Sonny."

Ben looks at me hard, but I hold his gaze. After a moment, his face softens. "Come on," he says, throwing an arm around my shoulder. "It's cold out here. Just come in for a minute. We need your help. If you don't like what we've got to say, you can leave."

I think about it for a minute. Part of me wants to leave right now to show him he can't control me the way Sonny controls him. But part of me wants to know what kind of help he needs. It's been a long time since Ben asked me for anything and a long time since he cared if I was around or not.

"Okay," I hear myself say. "But you gotta promise you'll come home with me when it's over. Mama's not feeling well, and it doesn't help when you keep her worried."

Ben scrunches up his face, considering my offer. "Deal," he says, and we go inside.

Sonny Abe's first name is Hiroshi. Like many kids born to Japanese parents, he has a Japanese name and an American name. At home he's called Hiroshi, but at school and in the town where he grew up outside of San Francisco, he was called Sonny. Sonny lives with his old grandfather, who is asleep already in the corner. Sonny's mother died when he was little, and his father was taken away by the FBI shortly after the Japanese attack on Pearl Harbor. Mr. Abe had been the head of the local Japanese Committee, and the FBI had arrested him along with other innocent men like him who held important positions in Japanese communities.

The FBI had sent Sonny's father to a special camp in North Dakota for "enemy aliens" to keep an eye on him. He caught pneumonia there and died, probably because he didn't have warm enough clothes. I've heard the story many times. It's a story Ben likes to tell when he's arguing with Papa about the injustices we've suffered. To me, though, Sonny is using his father's death as an excuse to act up. He reminds me of the toughs who'd stand on the street corners in Japantown, hassling little kids and stealing fruit from the street vendors. It's just that the war and the camps have given guys like Sonny bigger stakes to play with.

As soon as we enter the room, I notice that everyone here is calling Sonny "Hiroshi" now, and they greet my brother as Benjiro. When they ask about me, I speak up before Ben can. "My name is Tai." There are four other guys in the room. I recognize one as Shig's cousin, Yoshi. The others I don't know. If Sonny wasn't the leader of the attack on Mr. Sato, I wonder who was.

"So, Tai," Sonny says, drawing me toward the overturned crate that serves as a table. "Your brother tells us you're good with your hands."

I glance at Ben, who nods at me. "I guess so."

"Well, we need a shortwave radio. Think you can make us one?"

"We're not supposed to have shortwaves in camp."

"We're not supposed to have a lot of things in camp. Doesn't that get your goat, my friend?"

I cringe when he calls me that. "I don't wanna be part of your trouble."

"It's nothing bad, Tai," Ben insists. "We just want to be able to tune into Japanese radio broadcasts. We think the Caucasians aren't telling us the truth about how the war is going. We just wanna find out for ourselves."

He's looking me straight in the eye, and that's not something he can usually do if he's lying.

"What's the harm in a little radio?" Yoshi asks. "Maybe we can even get some music. You like music, don't you?"

I glare at Yoshi. I haven't forgotten what he did to Mr. Sato. "I'd need an AM radio so I can turn it into a shortwave."

"Yoshi has one," Ben says. "What else would you need?"

"Not much. But the antenna would be a problem.

You'd have to set it up outside the building."

Ben and Sonny exchange a glance. "We could do it at night," Sonny says. "We'll only put it up for a little while. No one will notice."

I shake my head. "It's too dangerous. Thanks to you guys, they're doing more searches on the barracks. What if they catch me making it?"

"You can make it here," Sonny says. "Then if there's trouble, I'll be the one who gets caught with it." The thought of hanging out at Sonny's gives me a sick feeling.

"I can't. I work at the newspaper after school, and after that Papa would want to know where I was."

"Tell him I'm helping you practice judo at the rec hall," Ben says. "I will too. I promise. We'll even invite Papa to come and watch us one time, so he doesn't suspect."

I stare at Ben for a moment. At first I'm tempted to take him up on his offer. I'd get my brother back in some small way, and he could help me beat Shig. But then I just get angry. He's using the one thing I care about right now, the judo tournament, to try to make me do what he wants. He doesn't really care if I win or not. He's only going to help me so I'll help him.

"Forget it," I say. "You want a shortwave so bad, make it yourself. Leave me out of it."

Ben reaches for me as I rush to leave. He follows me into the growing dark. "Tai, wait."

I keep my back to him. "You promised to come home now," I remind him.

"I will, in a minute. We got business to finish."

"Go ahead, then. Finish your business. It's not like I expect you to keep your promises anymore."

"Hey," he says.

"Why do you have to be like them, Ben? Why can't you be like you used to be?" I'm glad it's dark, so he can't see the tears in my eyes.

"Nothing's like it used to be, Tai. I don't expect Papa to understand that, but I thought you might. I thought I could *count* on you. It's just a stupid radio. That's all. You're the one who's making it out to be something more. Go home, *little brother*." This time he says it like I'm nothing more than a pain-in-the-neck kid. He goes back inside and slams the door.

I'm angry enough I feel like running, but there's nowhere to run. Then I feel like throwing something, but there's nothing to throw. So I kick the side of the barracks and immediately grab my foot. My toe is throbbing now, and I feel stupid. I start limping back toward Buck's apartment. But as I pass the newspaper office, I notice the light on. I wipe my eyes and peek in the window. It's Tom. He's bundled up and hunched over a typewriter. I push the door open and step in. It's cold in the office. Tom hasn't stoked the stove. When I ask him why, he says he doesn't plan to be here long. He just wants to type up his story for tomorrow and then get over to the school to help his brother build the backdrop for the talent show.

"Can I come with you?"

"Sure," he says. "How are you with microphones? We can't seem to get ours to work."

I smile. "I can fix it."

"You can?"

"Sure, I'm good with my hands, haven't you heard?" I say it with just enough sarcasm that he looks up from his story.

"You okay?"

I shrug. "Did you hear about Mr. Sato, Tom?"

"Yeah, I did. I stopped by the hospital earlier."

"How is he?"

"All right, I guess. Doc says he can go home tomorrow."

"Will they leave him alone now?"

"You'll have to ask your brother about that."

I bristle. "Ben had nothing to do with it."

Tom rips the paper from the typewriter and sets it on the desk. "Well, I hope not. You better steer clear of his crowd, though, Tai."

I pick up his story and pretend to read it. "Tom, how are you going to answer Questions 27 and 28 on the loyalty questionnaire?" I ask casually.

"Yes-yes, of course."

"I don't think my brother will. I think he'll sign no-no. You think that makes him a traitor?"

Tom stands up to face me. "Traitor's a harsh word, Tai. Ben's got some strong feelings, that's all. Lots of folks feel the same way. I guess we all gotta do what we think is best."

"What if he goes too far, Tom? What if the government ships him back to Japan? Some say they're going to do that with the folks who sign no-no."

"I don't think anyone will have to go to Japan unless they want to," Tom says, taking me by the shoulders and looking into my eyes. "Hasn't working at the paper taught you not to listen to rumors? If some of these folks want to go back to Japan, the government will let them. But no one's going to be forced to go. This is still America. We've still got rights."

"Doesn't feel like it sometimes."

Tom reaches up and pulls the cord on the single bulb that hangs from the center of the room. "It's a good country," Tom says. "Never give up on it, Tai. Once the war's over, this will all be behind us. Come on, let's get to the school. You sure you know how to fix a mic?"

"Piece of cake."

"See, I knew you were good for something."

As we hurry off toward the high school, I'm still thinking about Ben and Mr. Sato, and then Tom starts to sing a popular new song that's got everyone feeling patriotic. It's called "Comin' in on a Wing and a Prayer," and it's about a warplane that's been badly damaged in battle but is still hoping to make it home okay. I think Tom chose this song to cheer me up, or maybe he's trying to tell me that my problems could be worse than they are. He nudges me to sing along, but I shake my head. Still, the more he sings, the better I feel. Funny how songs can do that sometimes.

6

What Could It Hurt?

忠義

It's Friday night, and the mess hall is filling up fast. The high school talent show is tonight, and everyone is excited. The kids have been getting ready for it for weeks, and the old folks are anxious to spend an evening out of the barracks. I've been here the past two nights with Tom and his brother, setting things up backstage. Since I did such a good job fixing the mic the other day, the talent show committee put me in charge of it tonight. I have to make sure it doesn't come unplugged and try to keep the static down, but I also have to bring it on and off stage for the people who need it and adjust the height to suit them. I'm glad for the job. For one thing, I get to watch Kiomi rehearse. She's pretty in her white majorette dress with matching boots. I almost tell her so, but I chicken out.

Being at the rehearsals has also helped me keep my mind off Ben. We haven't spoken since I left

Sonny's. He didn't come home early that night as he'd promised. In fact, even with me stopping by the school with Tom, I still beat him home. I pretended to be asleep when he came in, so I wouldn't have to talk to him. I did the same thing last night, but, unlike my brother, I've never been good at holding grudges. Guess I take after Papa that way. It's not easy for me to hang onto my anger. Even tonight, I find myself hoping to see Ben's face in the crowd. He used to be quite the clown before the evacuation. He loved to sing off-key and tell jokes to make people laugh. When he was in seventh grade, he and a friend even won our school's talent show with Abbott and Costello's popular "Who's On First?" routine.

But as curtain time approaches, there's still no sign of Ben. Papa and Mama are in the audience, though. Mama is sitting with her friends from the Buddhist church, and Papa is standing along the wall with Tom and several other men. Tom says something that makes Papa laugh, and it's good to see the worry lines disappear from Papa's forehead for a moment.

I'm so focused on this scene I almost don't notice the curtain going up. Then the audience begins to clap, and I run out with the mic and set it in front of

Miss McAllister, the teacher in charge of the show. The first thing she does is lead us all in the Pledge of Allegiance. Everyone stands and lays a hand over their hearts. Then she welcomes us to the event and asks the kids sitting on the floor to scoot back a little from the stage. She apologizes to everyone for the heat in the room. One of the boys over-stoked the stove. Finally, she reminds us to save our clapping till the end of each routine. Then, without warning, she dashes off stage, leaving me scrambling to remove the mic before the majorettes began their routine. Kiomi doesn't drop the baton once, though each of the other girls does. And when their routine is over, she throws a big smile my way as she runs off the stage.

The rest of the show goes off with only a hitch here and there. By the time the curtain comes down for good, I'm sweating from the heat and the running around, but I'm happy. Everyone is. Fifteen minutes after the show ends, most of the participants and their families are still milling around congratulating each other. The senior girl who won first place is singing her song again just for fun, and Kiomi is showing her little cousin how to twirl the baton. Mama and Papa and I are chatting with our barracks neighbors, the Yamamotos, so when Ben comes rushing toward us, I feel my face break into a broad grin. But Ben doesn't return it. He pushes between us and the Yamamotos with only a cursory apology and draws Mama and Papa to the corner of the room. I follow.

"What is it, Benjiro?" Papa asks.

Ben's breath comes in ragged bursts and his cheeks are red. He must have been running to reach us. "It's Eiko," he says. "She had the baby."

Mama claps her hands, but Ben shakes his head. "It's not good, Mama. There were complications with the birth. The baby is fine, but Eiko . . ."

Mama covers her face. Papa reaches for the wall for support. Only I speak. "Eiko, *what*? Eiko what, Ben?"

"She didn't make it, little brother. She's gone."

My knees go weak, and I don't even try to reach a bench. I just drop down on the floor with my legs Indian style and let my head fall into my hands. I can hear Mama crying softly now and Papa saying to Ben, "Watch your brother. I'm taking your mother home."

Ben sits down beside me, so close that our shoulders touch. He doesn't say anything. I can hear people mumbling, and I know they're talking about us, wondering what's wrong. The front door opens and closes as the crowd quietly shuffles out. Someone pats my back, and I hear Tom say, "I'm sorry, Tai. Let me know if I can help." I see a pair of majorette boots stop in front of me, but I don't respond, and after a moment, the boots move away. When the room is finally quiet, I raise my head. The only two people left are Ben and me.

"Were you there when she died?"

"No. I was at our apartment picking up something when Mr. Hirata came by to give us the news."

I shake my head. "I can't believe she's gone. We just saw her. Well, you didn't," I say, and I can't help but sound a little mad. "She told me to bring you to the hospital when the baby was born because she hadn't seen you in so long."

"I saw her the other day, Tai. I went by after work to give her a rattle I made out of scrap lumber."

"You saw her? You made a rattle? I didn't know you could make toys."

"There's a lot you don't know about me," Ben says with a sad smile.

At that moment, I feel proud of my brother and

sorry I misjudged him. I should have known that as much as he's changed, he would never have forgotten Eiko. Thinking about her brings on my tears, and the lump in my throat makes it hard to talk. "Why did she die, Ben?"

Ben gives me an answer I don't expect. "Because she was in the camp."

"What do you mean?"

"If she'd been outside, at a *real* hospital, they could have saved her."

"You don't know that."

"Sure I do. They don't care what happens to us in here. I keep trying to tell you that."

I stare at my brother, wondering if what he's saying could be true. If maybe my cousin didn't have to die.

"They tell us what they want us to hear, Tai. It's like the way they call those dingy rooms we live in 'apartments' to make them sound better. Or the way they told us that coming to these camps was for our own protection, when we were perfectly safe in Sacramento. That was just a way for them to get our houses and crops and belongings for cheap. Yet we still believe everything they tell us. That's why Sonny and I wanted the shortwave. So we could get our own news and not have to rely on what the camp commanders tell us."

I look at my hands. I know I can make that shortwave. I made one once from parts I ordered from a catalog and a book I got for my birthday, and I remember how. I still don't believe Ben is right about everything. I think Tom's right about some things too. America is mostly a good country and President Roosevelt is mostly a good man. But even good men make mistakes. Maybe we do need to watch out for ourselves more, like Ben says. And what harm could a radio do? It's not like I'm helping him make a gun. Maybe if we all knew more about how the war's going, we could better show our support, and they'd let us out of here sooner. We could go home, and Papa could be a tofu maker and Mama could get better and we could all help care for Eiko's baby and Ben and I could quit arguing and just be brothers again.

I don't tell Ben I'm considering making the shortwave. I'm not even sure I can find the tools I need yet, and I'll have to figure out where to hide it while I'm working on it. My mind returns to Eiko, and I wonder what she would say about my plan. She'd tell me to forget it, that nothing is worth getting in trouble. But as my brother and I walk together toward home, I notice that we're moving in unison, our strides matching perfectly, and I imagine how surprised Ben will be if I can actually make him a shortwave. "Don't worry, Eiko," I think. "I'll be careful."

7

An Unwelcome Visit

忠義

Eiko had been right. The baby is a girl. She's tiny and wrinkled, with a shock of black hair sticking straight up. Dan named her Eiko, after her mother, and that made me glad. It was like a little piece of my cousin had lived on. When we went to pay our respects to Dan after Eiko's death, Ben came with us. He walked with Papa, and they talked about everything but their disagreements. It was nice to see them getting along again. When we got to Eiko's apartment, I stopped in the doorway. My feet wouldn't take me in. Guess I couldn't face that room again without Eiko's smiling face to greet me. I had the Lou Gehrig card in my back pocket. I still hadn't shown it to anyone. It was mine and Eiko's little secret.

Mama noticed me standing there and gently pulled me inside. She locked her arm through mine and guided me over to Mrs. Hirata, who was holding the baby for us to see. She handed the baby to Mama.

Ben reached over and pulled the pink blanket aside. He lay a finger on the baby's chest, and she grabbed it with her tiny hand. He looked up at Mama, and she smiled at him through her tears. I think it would have made Eiko happy to see how her baby brought my family together again.

Ben still goes to Sonny's each night, but he's been coming home a little earlier these past few days, which is good. Unrest is growing in camp, and Mama worries so much when Ben is out. Ever since Eiko's funeral, Ben has made an effort not to argue with Papa. They've even gone together several times to play cards with Dan to try to cheer him up.

As for me, Yoshi gave me his AM radio. I took it apart once already. I'm pretty sure I can make the adjustments to turn it into a shortwave. All I'll need is a soldering iron. I think I can get one from the electrician who let me borrow the tape I used to finally fix the loose wire at the newspaper office. He was the kind of guy who doesn't like to talk to kids. He just handed me the tape and never asked what I needed it for. Maybe he'll do the same with the iron. If he doesn't, I'll just have to sneak into his office when he's not around. If I put my mind to it, I can have that radio ready in no time.

Eiko's been gone for two weeks. It's Friday night again, and our neighbor, Mr. Yamamoto, has just come over with his Japanese *Go* board to play a game with Papa. Mrs. Yamamoto has brought her mending. She and Mama will be stitching all evening. Clothes wear out fast in camp, and we have so few of them. Mama is constantly mending. Ben is out, with Sonny no doubt, or maybe he's taken his new girlfriend to watch the movie at the mess hall. It's an old Tom Mix western, so I know Buck will be there too. He loves cowboy movies. But tonight Shig and I have judo practice. Now that things have settled down at home, I can concentrate on the tournament again.

Shig knocks on the door, and I dash out to meet him, forgetting to say good-bye to our guests. Mama will let me have it for that when I get home. Shig and I arrive at the recreation hall before anyone else, so we can get in some extra practice. Ben's been working with me on my *harai goshi* throw, and I'm eager to try it on Shig. As we roll out the mats, I tell him how Ben described that a good throw should feel light and effortless, but Shig doesn't answer me. When we get into position, I flip him easily.

"What's the matter with you tonight?" I ask. "You're not concentrating."

"Sorry, I've got a lot on my mind. Didn't your brother tell you they arrested my cousin Yoshi?"

"No, why?"

"There was another *inu* attack yesterday, and this time Yoshi led it."

"Not Mr. Sato again?" I say, feeling sick.

"No. Some young guy. Not much older than us. They say he lived near some of the No-No Boys over in Block 41, and he was telling the camp commander when the No-Nos were meeting."

I should have known things weren't really getting better. They never seem to these days. I was glad Shig hadn't mentioned my brother being involved. He must have been at work again when it happened.

"Did the MPs get Sonny too?"

"Nah. Sonny's too smart. He plans all this stuff, but he makes the other guys do the dirty work so he won't get caught."

"Well, maybe the jail's a good place for Yoshi," I say, not really thinking about what I'm saying. "Tom says sometimes the best thing to do with traitors is to keep them away from everyone else."

"Who says Yoshi's a traitor?"

"Well, everybody knows he hates America. I mean, he was one of the first to sign no-no."

"Then I guess that makes your brother a traitor too."

I tense. Even though I've wondered about that myself, it's different when someone else says it. "My brother's no traitor, Shig. We still don't know what Ben signed on the questionnaire. He hasn't said."

"Oh come on, Tai. Everyone knows he runs with the No-Nos."

I'm feeling bad about starting this fight, but I still can't let him talk down about my brother. "Drop it, Shig."

"No, this is good to know, Tai. So you think all No-Nos are traitors except your brother? So I guess that means you'd think my father's a traitor too?"

"What are you talking about?"

"My father signed no-no on the form."

"He did? Why?!"

"With all the trouble here, there are rumors that people who sign yes-yes are going to get moved to other camps in Utah or Idaho or maybe as far away as Arizona. Dad's afraid if we leave California, we might never be able to afford to come back. So he signed no-no so they'd keep us at Tule Lake."

"But that makes your family disloyal!"

In a flash, Shig has me on the ground and is sitting

on my chest, his hands digging into my shoulders as he pins me down. "We are not disloyal!" he shouts, his face next to mine.

"Boys!" our Sensei yells. He pulls Shig off of me, and I jump to my feet. The other boys have gathered around. I feel a heat rising in me and wish I could lash out at something too. But Sensei is holding Shig by the arm, and the expression on Sensei's face makes it clear he won't tolerate any more fighting. Shig is still shaking with anger as he yanks his arm away from Sensei.

I probably shouldn't have said what I did. It's not Shig's fault his father signed no-no, and I've known Shig's dad all my life. There's nothing disloyal about him. Maybe he just did what he thought he had to, like Ben is doing. I take a step toward Shig, but he storms out of the barracks. He doesn't even take his coat. Some of the younger kids snicker, and I fix them with my meanest glare. They go back to their own mats to practice.

Sensei finds another boy for me to spar with, but my mood has soured, and the boy pins me easily. I lie on my back looking up at the row of bare light bulbs hanging from the barracks's ceiling, hating this camp. I've tried to be like my father, to accept what's happening to us without complaint. I've tried to just focus on the things I love, like sports and my friends, but sometimes it feels like everything I care about is being taken away from me. First my home and my things, then my brother and Eiko, now Shig. Even Mama's no longer the same, half the time sick, her smile harder to find these days. And now if Shig is right, if the government is going to separate the yes-yes families from the no-nos, we could be moving again. This time I'll lose Shig for sure, and who knows where Buck's family will wind up. It's amazing, isn't it, how sometimes in a room full of people, you can still feel so alone?

After practice, some of the older kids head over to the canteen. They ask if I want to come, but I'm in no mood. I get one of them to agree to take Shig his coat. I'll talk to Shig tomorrow when he cools off. Right now I just want to get home. If my parents are still distracted with the neighbors, I might be able to work on the radio. When I get to the barracks, the scene is the same as when I left—Papa and Mr. Yamamoto at the *Go* board, Mama and Mrs. Yamamoto at their mending—but they've saved me a piece of licorice that the Yamamotos brought to share. "*Arigato gozaimasu*," I remember to say this time, as I bow quickly. Then I cross over to my side of the room and close the divider. I crawl into my bunk, sitting with my back to the curtain, and drape the covers around my shoulders so they hide the radio. I sit cross-legged with the radio in front of me, but I also lay my copy of *Oliver Twist* in my lap. If one of my parents comes in, I can hold up my book as if I've been reading.

Sonny lent me the pocketknife he smuggled into camp, so I can strip the insulation off the wires. It makes me nervous having the knife around—we're not supposed to have them—but it's the best tool for this job. I hear a knock on the door. It's nine o'clock, and I wonder who would be calling so late. I jump out of bed and yank the covers over the knife and radio. Papa has answered the door, and a big Caucasian man in a dark suit is standing on the doorstep. I immediately think of the shortwave and the knife. If this is a raid, I'm in big trouble.

My heart is pounding, but then I notice it's just the man in the suit and no MPs. If this were a raid, he'd have brought the military police with him. Mr. Sato is standing behind the man in the suit, and he nods at me. I feel my breath release, but I stand in front of the divider just to make sure no one comes in. As Mr. Sato enters, I notice he's still hunched over from the broken ribs he got when Sonny's boys beat him. Mama and Mrs. Yamamoto quickly clear the table, and Papa offers the Caucasian man a cup of coffee. "No thank you, sir," he says. He and Mr. Sato sit down at our lopsided table across from Papa. Mr. Sato and the man in the suit have their backs to me, but I can see Papa's face clearly. He gives me a faint smile.

Papa turns to Mr. Sato first and says in Japanese, "I'm surprised you're still working for the Caucasians. Aren't you afraid after what the No-Nos did to you?"

"I only came because it was you, my friend," Mr. Sato says. "I was careful. I had him meet me here, so no one would see us walking together."

Papa nods his appreciation and turns his attention to the man in the suit.

"Sorry to call so late," the camp official says, and Mr. Sato translates his words into Japanese for my parents. "Now, don't worry. There's no concern," the man goes on. "I'm just here to talk to you about the *Dispatch.*"

"The newspaper?" Papa asks.

"Yeah. We know you write some articles in

Japanese for the older folks, the ones who don't read English. Now, I'm not here to say you can't do that. Have no fear of that. I'm just here to make sure we understand each other."

"What do you mean?" Papa asks through Mr. Sato.

"Well, there's a lot of folks been feeling some sympathy toward enemy nations these days. You know I mean Japan, don't you?"

Papa nods. It's a good thing the man has his back to me, because I can't help screwing up my face. He's talking to my father like he's a child.

"So the camp commander just wants to make sure you're not helping fuel that fire, you know? That means making matters worse. We need to make sure your articles aren't about things that might raise concerns. I'm sure we need have no fear of that. Am I right?"

Papa's upper lip twitches like he wants to say something, but all he does is nod. He even lowers his eyes as a sign of respect, but that lip still twitches, and I wish he *would* say something. I wish he'd tell this overgrown buffoon that he's barking up the wrong tree. That he's talking to a man who's so loyal his own son will barely speak to him sometimes.

"Well, I'm glad we understand each other, Mr.

Shimoda," the man in the suit says. "Thank you, Mr. Sato, for your help. I'll just see myself out, folks." As he opens the door, I catch a glimpse of two MPs standing outside, their rifles thrown over their shoulders, and I realize if Papa hadn't given the right answer they might have taken him away. He was right to keep his mouth shut. I think about what I said to Shig and wish I could keep my mouth shut too.

A minute passes. None of us say anything. The walls in the barracks are thin, and if the man and his MPs are still outside, they might overhear us. Finally Papa goes back to the corner of the room. He stands with his back to us, studying the *Go* board. His fists are clenched and his eyes closed. He's taking deep breaths, working to pull his anger in the way he always does. When I see his shoulders slacken, I feel my own body relax.

But then my father's hand shoots out, and the *Go* board and all its pieces clatter noisily across the floor.

8

The Last Straw

忠義

After the Yamamotos leave, Papa orders me to bed. I feel anything but tired, but I can see Papa's in no mood to argue. He's pacing back and forth in the front part of our room. I clear the radio and knife off my cot and put them back in their hiding places. I tell Papa I'm going to the latrine and I'll be right back. He grunts at me in response. On my way, I look for Ben. I wonder if I should tell him what happened or if that would just make matters worse. I'm relieved when I don't find him, but I'm busting to tell somebody. I still feel that way the next morning, so I get up early and run to Shig's apartment before school. I've brought a peace offering, a piece of black licorice Mrs. Yamamoto left for me. One of Shig's little sisters answers my knock. She sees the candy and squeals with delight. She snatches it from my hand as Shig reaches the door.

"Hey," I call out, "that's for your brother."

Shig just shrugs. "Ah let her have it."

He's not mad anymore. I can tell. Good old Shig. If it were Buck, he wouldn't speak to me for a week.

"Sorry about yesterday," I say.

"Forget it."

"No. I shouldn't have said what I said. I know your family's not disloyal."

"Thanks."

He may not be mad anymore, but I can tell by the tightness in his voice that he's still holding back.

"Can I tell you something?" I ask. "In private."

That gets him curious. "I'll get my stuff." A minute later, he follows me into the cold morning air. February is turning into March, and the wind is picking up.

"What's up? Is it your brother?" Shig asks.

"No, my dad."

He's all ears now. I tell him all about the man in the suit's visit and how my father reacted. By the time I've finished the story, we're nearing the high school. Shig pulls me over beside one of the barracks. "Now can I tell *you* something?"

"Shoot."

He glances around then lowers his voice. "My cousin Yoshi's back. They only kept him for a few hours as a warning. He says your brother is planning to steal a radio from the camp commander's office. Ben and Sonny are working the whole thing out."

"What? No! I'm making him a shortwave radio. He doesn't have to steal one. He'll get caught!"

"You're doing what?"

"I'm making him a radio. You can't tell anyone. Not even Buck."

"So now you're in on this too?"

"No. I'm just trying to help Ben a bit. They're not going to use it for anything bad. They just want to try to hear some broadcasts from Japan. Honest, Shig. It's nothing."

Shig shakes his head. "This whole thing is getting out of hand. Someone threw a rock through our neighbor's window last night. And our neighbor's a No-No, so that means some of the Loyals are acting up now too."

"It'll all settle down soon," I say.

"You can't get involved, Tai. It's too dangerous."

"I won't. I promise. I'll just finish the radio and that's it."

"What's it?" Buck asks, ambling toward us.

I look to see what Shig will say, but he keeps my secret.

"Just talkin' 'bout homework, Buck," Shig says. "Nothing *you'd* know anything about."

"Speaking of that, which one of you fellas wants to help me with my English paper tonight?"

"That would be Tai," Shig says. It's his way of letting me know I owe him a favor.

"All right, Buck," I sigh. "Come to my place after school, and we'll get started."

"Thatta boy," Buck says, dropping an arm across my shoulders. "Have you seen Kiomi this morning? She was asking for you yesterday."

"She was?"

"Nah, why would she ask for *you*?"

I elbow him in the gut, and he grabs his side, laughing. "Ain't you ever gonna talk to her, Tai? Should I call her over for ya?" he chides, as Shig and I head off toward the school. "Ah come on, fellas. Wait up!"

Buck and I walk back toward my apartment after school. He wants to stop off at the camp store first to buy a snack. Buck is always thinking about food. He buys us a box of Red Hots to share and a box of Kellogg's Corn Flakes for himself. He eats the cereal straight out of the box. While we're in the store, we poke around at the other items. There's a long, wooden table piled with shirts and sweaters and dresses. Throw rugs hang from the rafters. Blankets are piled at the back of the store. Canned or boxed foods, at least the ones that are available, are on shelves that line the outside of the store. It's always busy in here, people pushing past each other. There's not much else to do in camp. Some folks come nearly every day just to see if anything new has arrived. I usually see some of the kids from school here, but not today.

"Come on, I'm bored," I say to Buck, and we leave. We're chewing on Red Hots and shooting a rubber band back and forth at each other when we approach my barracks. I'm so distracted waiting for the rubber band to hit that I don't hear my father and brother going at it till I'm inside the door. Buck hears it then too. He stops and picks up the rubber band that just ricocheted off my neck and hands it to me. I wrap it around my wrist. He shrugs at me, wondering if he should come in. I close the door and whisper, "Why don't you head over to your place. I'll meet you there soon." Buck nods and shuffles off. I take a deep breath and step inside. Mama meets me at the door and helps me off with my coat.

"So you signed no-no then?" Papa is saying.

Ben draws himself to his full height. He's taller than Papa now by an inch or two. "Yes, I did."

"*Baka*! Do you know what you've done, Benjiro?"

"I've stood up for what I believe in."

"You've broken up this family." Ben stiffens, but Papa continues, "You'll have to stay in Tule Lake now until the war is over, and we'll go on."

"You don't know that, Papa," I interrupt. "Maybe we can stay here too."

"No, Taichirou. If the government lets us, we're leaving."

"But we can't leave Ben."

"Ben has made his choice. He is no longer part of this family." He makes a swiping motion like he's cutting something away.

"What do you mean, Papa?" I ask, my voice breaking.

Papa turns to Ben. "I asked you to honor my wishes. I asked you to sign yes-yes on the oath. Is it so much to ask a son to be loyal to his family, to his country? You have disgraced us, Benjiro."

"Papa!"

"This does not concern you, Tai." Papa turns back

to Ben, and there's a hardness in his face I've never seen before. "You are eighteen now. You're a man. You can live with the other bachelors. You should go now."

Mama gasps. She nudges me, but there's nothing I can do. Papa's voice is firm. I look at Ben instead, my eyes pleading, hoping he'll say something to get Papa to change his mind. "I'll stay at Sonny's tonight," he says. "And make arrangements to move tomorrow."

He throws his shaving kit and some clothes into his duffel bag and pauses only to glance at Mama before he heads outside. Mama is standing behind me, her hands on my shoulders. I pull away from her and follow Ben. I have to run to keep up with him.

"Ben?" He doesn't stop. "Ben, wait." He keeps going. I sprint to get ahead of him and block his path. "Don't steal the radio."

"How'd you know about that?"

"Never mind how I know. Just don't do it. I've got a radio for you. It's almost done. I can get it to you tomorrow."

Ben lowers the duffel bag to the ground and crosses his arms. "You swear?"

"Yeah."

"Does it work?"

"It should."

"Okay, bring it by Sonny's tomorrow night." He picks up his bag again and maneuvers around me.

"Ben?" I trot to keep up with him. "Don't worry, okay? Papa will get over it. You'll be back home soon."

Ben shakes his head. "You've got a lot to learn, Tai. As Papa said, I'm eighteen now. I can do what I want. Heck, I might even go back to Japan with Chiyo's family."

I pull on his arm till he stops again. "Who's Chiyo? Your girlfriend?"

"Yeah. She's giving up her American citizenship, and her family is going back to Japan."

I try to think about what this means. It was bad enough to think Ben might be a few states away; now he's talking about an ocean away. "You wouldn't really do that, would you, Ben? You wouldn't leave America?"

"I don't know. Maybe," he says, but for the first time in weeks, he sounds unsure. That gives me hope. I step aside to let him pass.

"Hey, little brother," he says over his shoulder, "don't forget to work on *osaewaza*. You were right, you know? If you're going to beat Shig, you're going to have to get better at the hold-downs."

"I will," I say, and my brother turns the corner out of sight.

Later that night, when we're all in bed, I hear my mother crying, just as she did when we first came to camp. After a time, though, the room goes quiet, except for the snoring coming from the Yamamoto apartment next door. I'm lucky there's no moon tonight. It'll make it easier not to be seen as I sneak over to Sonny's. I tuck the radio and the wire for the antenna under my coat and pull on my shoes. As I pass my father's bed, he raises his head, "Where are you going, Tai?"

"To the latrine," I say, keeping my voice as steady as I can.

"Can't you wait until morning?"

"No. My stomach hurts. I may be a while."

I can feel Papa's eyes on me in the dark. "Okay," he says at last, and I hurry outside. I run as fast as I can to Block 30, where Sonny lives, and knock on the door. Sonny answers. I hold my coat shut tight, so he can't see anything. "Is Ben here?" I ask.

"Did you bring the radio?"

I should have known Ben would tell him. He tells Sonny everything these days. I try to peer around Sonny at Ben, but Sonny blocks the door. "Give me the radio."

"I want to see my brother first," I say.

Sonny considers this for a moment, then lets me in. Ben is sitting in a scrap-wood chair in the corner. He's been trying to sleep sitting up. He looks exhausted, but he rises to greet me.

I pull the radio and the antenna wire out from under my coat and lay them on the table.

"I knew you could do it," Ben says.

"I don't know if it can pick up Japanese broadcasts," I say. "You'll have to play with it. Try different frequencies. But, Ben, if anyone sees the antenna—"

"Let us worry about that," Sonny says, taking me by the collar and leading me toward the door. "You better get home before someone misses you."

I look to Ben to stand up for me, but he's dropped back down in the chair, his eyes closed. I realize then he doesn't look well. He's pale, and his forehead is beaded with sweat. There's a bout of influenza going around camp, and I wonder if Ben could have it.

"Is my brother okay?" I ask Sonny as he pushes me out the door.

"Yeah, yeah. He's fine. I'll take care of him. You just remember to keep your mouth shut about the radio."

"Who would I tell?" I snap. "I'm the one who made it, remember? You think I wanna get myself in trouble?"

"That's right. You could get yourself in trouble." He smirks at me.

"Take care of my brother," I say, but Sonny just closes the door in my face. I hope I was right to give Ben and Sonny the radio. It seemed like such a harmless thing when I made it, but the way Sonny looked tonight, I wonder what he's really up to. And I wonder if he'll really take care of my brother.

I wish I could tell Mama about Ben. Maybe she could check on him or insist Papa let him come home until he's well. But I better not. Mama has enough worries, and Ben would be furious if I brought her to Sonny's. I'll just check on him tomorrow myself, Sonny or no Sonny.

9

The Arrest

忠義

I didn't see Ben yesterday after all. I stopped by Sonny's apartment after school, but no one answered my knock. Maybe I was wrong about Ben being sick. Maybe he was just tired, or maybe they've moved him to his new unit already. I keep an eye out for him today as I walk back and forth from our block to school and to the newspaper and home. I even poke into a few latrines to see if he's working, but there's no sign of him. Hard to believe anyone can disappear in a fenced-in camp, but it's not that difficult in our little city to hide if you want to. They're serving beef sukiyaki tonight, kind of their take on a Japanese dish, with steamed rice and potato salad. Mama will be happy to have the rice. It goes so much easier on her stomach. I'm eating with my friends tonight, but I can see Mama and Papa and the Yamamotos at another long table. And Mr. Sato with his family eating with the reverend of our Buddhist church.

Shig is scraping his tin plate with his fork, and the noise makes my teeth hurt, like fingernails on a chalkboard. I reach across and grab his hand. "Stop it."

"Stop what?"

"Quit scraping your fork. It's annoying."

"Since when?"

"Since always."

Buck leans across and stabs a piece of beef off my plate. "What's your problem tonight?" he asks.

I tuck my plate in closer, out of his reach. "Nothing."

"He's been all balled up since his brother moved out," Shig says.

"Shut up," I say. I've got the sudden urge to get away from everyone, go for a walk, maybe by the perimeter where I can see Castle Rock outside the camp. Just be alone, you know. But just then, one of the kids from school comes skidding up to our table.

"Hey, fellas, I just saw the MPs headed for Sonny's quarters. Think there's gonna be trouble?"

"Nah, probably just a contraband raid," Buck says, and my stomach lurches.

I glance across the table at Shig. He seems to think of the radio at the same time I do. We both jump up. “Hey, where you goin’?” Buck asks, shoving a last bite of rice in his mouth and following.

We run as fast as we can to Sonny’s block. As we round the corner of the barracks, we see the MPs. Two have Ben by the arms, another is holding the radio. Sonny is nowhere in sight. My brother is hunched over. His head droops. I wasn’t wrong. He is sick, but he’s also defiant. When they talk to him, he doesn’t answer. One of them whacks him in the back of the head. I move forward, but Shig pulls me back.

“What do you think they’ll do to him?” I ask.

“They’ll question him first. Maybe he’ll tell them he just wanted the radio to listen to music. They’ll go easy on him then.”

“What radio?” Buck asks.

I ignore him. “What if he doesn’t, though? What if he tells them he was trying to hear Japanese broadcasts?”

“Then they might take him to the jail. Can you blame them though? They can’t let folks get away with breakin’ every rule.”

“I can’t believe you’re siding with the *hakujin*.”

“I’m not! But what did you think would happen? Did you think Ben could keep a radio hidden for long in this camp?”

"*What* radio?" Buck repeats.

I glare at him. "Never mind. I need to find my father."

I leave Buck and Shig standing at the corner, Buck still bugging Shig to tell him what's going on. I run all the way back to the mess hall, but my parents have left. So I head for our unit, but they aren't there, either. I check at the Yamamotos and wonder if I should run as far as Dan's unit. Then I remember where Mama is. She's meeting some other women at the Buddhist church to knit socks for the soldiers. So that means Papa is on his own. Where would he go if not to Mr. Yamamoto's? The newspaper! I run to the office. Sure enough, he's there, and so is Tom. They're at separate typewriters, working on their stories. Neither is talking. Tom doesn't speak much Japanese. He seems happy to see me when I come in, but I hesitate. I hadn't planned on anyone else hearing about Ben. But it's Tom. Maybe he can help.

"Hey ya, Tai," Tom says. My father looks up when he hears my name. I bend over to catch my breath, and Papa comes to my side.

"Somethin' wrong?" Tom asks.

"The MPs took Ben," I say. "He had a shortwave radio. They arrested him." I repeat it to my father in

Japanese. I wait for him to ask me more, but he just quietly closes the door behind me.

"We need to help him," I say to my father in Japanese. "We need to help him," I say again to Tom. Tom fixes his gaze on the typewriter. My father goes back to his paper.

"Well?" I say. "What should we do?" But neither of them answer me.

"Ben is sick, Papa. I saw him. He's got the flu or something. We should help him."

For a moment, I think I read sympathy in my father's eyes, but then he shakes his head. "Ben is a grown man now. He must learn from his own mistakes."

"So you want to see him go to jail?"

"*Deru kui wa utareru*" he says. It's an expression. It means "the stake that sticks out gets hammered down." It's what he's always told us about going along with things, not making waves. I guess he feels it's time Ben learned that lesson for himself.

I turn to Tom instead. "Tom?"

"Sorry, Tai. This is Ben's battle."

"Arghh!" I yell. Why does everyone have to be so stubborn? I hit the door with my fist, and immediately my knuckles begin to bleed.

Papa sighs. He takes a handkerchief out of his pocket and wraps it around my hand. "This is hard for you, I know." He lays a hand on my shoulder. "But you must think of your mother, Tai. If your brother is with the No-Nos, his problems will only get worse. The worry makes your mother sick."

I understand what he's saying, but I think even my mother would want us to help Ben. "Fine," I say. "If you won't help him, I'll find someone who will."

As I rush outside, I hear Tom calling for me. I stop, but I don't turn around. I wait for him to catch up to me. "Where'd he get the radio, Tai?" Tom asks.

I shrug.

"There's all kinds of loyalty, Tai. It's good that you want to be loyal to your brother, but what about your parents? What about your country? You can't help Ben right now. He has to help himself. There's been a lot of talk in this camp about loyalty lately. Now you have to figure out where *your* loyalty lies."

I glare at him. This is none of his business anyway. How would he know what I'm feeling? It's easy for him. He simply signed yes-yes and that was it. He even enlisted for the army. When the army calls him up, he'll go and fight for this country, even though it locked us up in this crummy camp. He says that's the only way to prove to the Caucasians how loyal we really are.

Everything's clear to Tom, but it's not clear to Ben, and now it's not clear to me. I don't want to disobey my father, but in Japanese tradition, an older brother deserves respect too. Figure out where your loyalties lie, Tom said, but how do I do that? Everyone's right. Tom's right and Ben's right and even my stubborn father is right. And they're all wrong too. But I can't just leave my sick brother alone. I have to find Sonny.

When I see Sonny, he's sitting at a table in the canteen with a girl on either side of him. He's laughing loud and talking big, like he always does. In that moment, I remember how much I dislike him, and I remember that he's the one who got Ben into this mess. But now he might be the only one who can get him out.

I walk over to the table, and when Sonny's eyes meet mine, he smirks. "Well, if it isn't Little Brother."

"Don't call me that." Sonny's friends laugh. "Where's Ben?" I ask.

"Don't know. In for questioning, probably."

"Did you check on him?" I ask Sonny.

"Do you think I want to show my face around the MPs?" Sonny asks.

"But you promised to take care of him."

"Ah they won't keep him long. He's smart. He'll talk his way out of it."

"You said you'd say the radio was yours."

"Well now, I wasn't home was I?"

"Yeah," I say. "You never seem to be home when the trouble starts."

One of Sonny's friends scoots his chair away and starts to stand. I step back.

"Leave it," Sonny says. "You better beat it, kid. You're getting on my nerves."

I look into each of the faces that surround Sonny and find no sympathy in any of them. I wish Ben could see this. I wish he could see what his "friends" are really like.

It's growing dark as I approach the gate that leads to the administration building, but when I get there, I hesitate. I'm afraid to go through. If they ask me questions about the radio, I'm not sure I'll be able to lie. I pace back and forth, trying to figure out what to do, trying to think of someone else who can help, but there isn't anyone. Finally, I sit down outside the gate and wait. A few minutes later, Ben stumbles by. He's clasping his coat tight across his chest and coughing heavily. I run to help him, but he shakes me off.

"You okay?" I ask.

"I'm fine. I just wanna get away from here."

"Where should we go?"

"I don't know, just go."

So we walk. We walk past row after row of barracks, past little garden areas the evacuees have just begun to plot out, past smelly latrines and laundry rooms, past a mess hall. Ben is moving slowly and coughing a lot, but he doesn't stop until we reach the warning fence, where the bored guard in the watchtower turns toward us. Ben grabs hold of the low fence with both hands and makes like he's going to jump it.

"Step back," the guard yells from his tower.

Ben ignores him.

The guard raises his rifle and yells, louder this time, "Step back or I'll shoot."

I reach for Ben's coat and yank him back. There are tears running down his face, and he coughs so heavily that I make him sit down. Beyond the barbed-wire fence is an ever-darkening sky and dead, dry grass and scrub-brush and broken seashells and miles and miles of nothing, and part of me wants to leave Tule Lake for another camp just to get away from this place, but Ben couldn't come with us. He'll have to stay with the rest of the No-Nos.

"Do you think they've forgotten us?" I ask.

"Who?"

"The people on the outside?"

"They were glad to see us go. Never liked us anyway," Ben says.

"We had Caucasian friends back in Sacramento."

"Yeah, a few. But there were just as many people who hated us and always did. That's why they passed the laws to keep us from owning land and to keep our parents from becoming citizens. That's why we're in these camps and people with German parents or Italian parents aren't, even though we're fighting their homelands too. It's not as easy to spot a German as it is a Jap. It isn't just that we've been abandoned," Ben says. "It's that they never wanted us in the first place."

Ben coughs heavily. I take a chance and pat his back. To my surprise, he lets me. I realize this must be what Ben's been feeling all along. Abandoned. His good friends went to other camps, and his plans to get a job or go to college were taken from him, and when they rounded us up, he couldn't even do what other young men were doing. He couldn't join the fight, even though he was *Nisei*, born right here in the United States. No one wanted him until Sonny came along, and now Sonny's turned on him. And what about me? Didn't I just let him down too?

"I'm sorry I didn't come in to help you, Ben," I say quietly.

"It's all right."

"I was scared."

"I know. Me too."

"What did you tell them?"

"Don't worry. I didn't tell them about you, Tai."

"That's not what I meant. Are you still in trouble?"

"I don't think so. I told them I didn't know it was a shortwave. That I found it in a latrine I was cleaning and thought it was just a regular radio. I think I looked so sick and pitiful they believed me. Then they let me go."

"You should come home with me now," I say.

"I don't think so, Tai."

"But you're sick. I can scrounge you up some food."

"I'm fine. Thanks for your help."

"But—"

"It's okay, Tai. Go home. Really. Go home."

As I turn away, the guard in his tower leans over the ledge to watch me. I glance back at Ben. He's slumping away in the other direction, toward his new quarters. It's not too far. He'll be fine, I tell myself. He likes to do things on his own. But then I get a picture of him standing here behind this fence after Papa and Mama and I have moved on. And in that picture, he looks so alone.

10

What Do You See?

忠義

It's late Saturday morning, and I'm still in bed. There's no reason to get up. It's raining, and there's nothing to do anyway. I pull the covers up and roll over. I haven't seen Ben since I left him by the fence four days ago. I've gone by his new apartment a few times, but he's never there. Shig says he saw him yesterday at the latrine and that he looked better, but Ben hasn't come by to see us yet. Papa's been very quiet these past few days. He doesn't look at me much, and I don't look at him. I'm still mad at him for not helping Ben. My friends have been avoiding me too. They say I'm mopey, but all Buck wants to talk about is girls and movies, and all Shig wants to do is practice judo. How can I expect my friends to understand? Their families are still together. They don't have the kinds of problems I do.

My father is still insisting we leave if we get the chance. He says if they don't move us, maybe he'll apply for a sponsor to hire us to work in the unrestricted areas outside of California. He keeps saying it's for Mama's sake, but I think there's something more. He hasn't gotten over the shame of the camp official's visit. He quit helping at the newspaper yesterday because he couldn't stand thinking twice about what he wrote anymore. I think that whole experience and all the trouble with the No-Nos has soured him on this camp. He's convinced himself things will be better somewhere else. Who knows, maybe they will. I've heard there aren't very many Japanese in states like Utah or Idaho, unlike California. Maybe they don't know enough to hate us there.

I'm still lying in bed when Mama peeks her head around the divider. "Get up, Tai," she says. "You missed breakfast."

"I'm not hungry."

She moves fully into my side of the room now. "Get up."

I groan and slide my feet to the floor. "You will come with me today," she says.

"Where?"

"I got us a day pass."

I sit up. It's been a while since I've been out

of camp. They don't give day passes out too easily anymore. "How'd you get the pass?"

"I told the officer we need to go over by Castle Rock to find good seashells for a gift for baby Eiko. Not these broken shells you find in camp."

"And he believed you?"

"Of course. It's not far. And what would he think? That we were going to walk all the way back to Sacramento?"

I shrug, but Mama slaps me lightly on the shoulder to get me moving. She's saved me some toast from breakfast, which she heats over the potbelly stove while I get dressed. I chew the dry toast slowly, until she pushes me off the bench and out the door. She waits while I visit the latrine and splash some water on my face. I walk with her to the gate, where we show our pass to the guard and stick close to the fence till we reach the edge of the camp. Folks in camp call Castle Rock a mountain, but it isn't really a mountain. It's more like a hill, but it's enough of a walk that I grumble about the effort. Mama ignores me.

Japanese mothers don't talk much to their children. They don't hug and kiss their kids a lot, like I see the Caucasian women doing, but we know they love us. Today Mama and I walk side by side, but with a good distance between us. She's quiet for the whole walk. When we finally reach the base of the hill, we scour it for seashells and find a few whole ones. Mama wraps each of them in a scrap of cloth and puts them in a basket she borrowed from Mrs. Yamamoto. She carries it carefully. After about an hour, she suggests we climb up the mountain a ways. I don't want to. I want to sit down and do nothing, but she prods me on. I walk ahead of her, stopping from time to time to give her a hand up. When we get about halfway up, she sits down for a rest and I join her. We can see for miles in every direction, and we can see the camp sprawling before us. I'm staring ahead, not thinking of anything, when Mama says, "What do you see, Tai?"

"A stupid, old camp."

"Hmm. What else do you see?"

"I see Eiko's grave."

"What else?"

"Dust."

"What else?"

I groan, but she nudges me, so I look a little deeper. "I see rows of ugly barracks with tarpaper sides."

"What else?"

"Too many people."

"What else?"

"Ah Mama."

"What else, Tai?"

I look a little deeper still. She's not gonna stop till I say something good, so I look for something I like. "I see kids playing. I see the basketball nets."

"Uh-huh. See the school?" Mama says.

"Yeah, but that's not good."

Mama smiles. She sits down close to me. "Do you know what I see, Tai? I see those ugly barracks too, but I see the gardens our people have planted next to them. Pretty gardens that will have flowers and rocks and vegetables. I see women coming out of the general store with fabric for new dresses. I see old men playing checkers and children playing tag. I see young couples preparing to get married. I see families, Tai. Lots of families." She leans into me slightly. "I see a people who have suffered much but kept their dignity and their honor. What happens to us doesn't matter. It's *who we are* that matters."

When I look again, I can almost see what Mama is seeing. I see people lining up early outside the mess halls for lunch, laughing and talking. I see women hanging laundry to dry on the clotheslines and men on the construction crews putting up new buildings and fixing leaky roofs. I see Caucasian men and women who've come to camp on their weekend to teach classes in sewing or American history, and I see young men raking smooth the baseball diamond for the afternoon game. I can pick out our block way off in the middle of camp and imagine Shig and Buck heading over for lunch and Kiomi thinking about what she'll wear to the dance tonight. I imagine Papa playing *Go* with Mr. Yamamoto and Tom working on a story.

"Do you know what else I see, Tai?" Mama says. "I see two brothers, each very different, each very strong, and a father who loves them both."

I groan again. Mothers always have to take things one step too far.

She takes a deep breath and asks, "Do you really want to stay here with Ben if we leave?"

"I don't know."

"I want you to come with us," she says, "but I don't think your father will force you to go."

"Are you saying I can decide for myself?"

"Maybe."

I glance at her, but her eyes are fixed on Mount

Shasta, way off in the distance. She's clasping her hands together tightly in her lap. We sit in silence for a moment, then I think she swipes at a tear before she drops the basket in my lap. "Let's go," she says, hopping up before I can even move. She starts picking her way down the path, and as I watch her quick, steady steps, I want to give something back to her. I try to think of something a mother would want to hear. I catch up to her on the path.

"Mama, Ben has a girlfriend."

"I know."

"How do you know?"

She just smiles.

"Her name is Chiyo."

"Hmm."

"Her family is going back to Japan. She wants Ben to go too."

"He won't."

"How do you know?"

"I know." She says firmly.

"She's tall," I say.

"Hmm."

"And pretty,"

"Kiomi is pretty also," she says, and I stumble. How does she know about Kiomi?

I keep my gaze straight ahead, but I see her out of the corner of my eye. She's smiling again.

When we get back, I'm suddenly very hungry. I run to the mess hall for lunch and find Shig and Buck inside. They share their food with me, since they've already stopped serving. It's macaroni and cheese, a dish even the army can't ruin. We chat excitedly about the basketball game that afternoon. We're playing the team from our rival block, and we're hoping to trounce them like we did last time.

Tom walks by, headed out. He sees me and raises an eyebrow in my direction. It's a look that asks if he and I are okay. I wave him over.

"You comin' to the dance tonight?" Tom asks.

"Wouldn't miss it," I say. Woody Ichihashi's band, The Downbeats, are playing. They're the best in camp. Everyone loves them, even my mother.

"Good. We need somebody to help set up the band. Can you come early?"

"Sure. I'll head over after the basketball game."

"Make sure you clean up first," Tom says. "You never know which girls might be lookin' your way.

Oh hey, I almost forgot. I got a note for you from Ben."

"Ben? When did you see him?"

"He came by the newspaper yesterday afternoon to find you. I told him I'd give it to you next time I saw you." Tom hands me a crumpled piece of paper with something typed on one side and something written on the other. "Sorry 'bout the paper," Tom says. "We can't spare too much, so I had to give him a piece I'd typed an old story on."

"That's all right," I say, unfolding the note quickly. In Ben's loopy handwriting, it says, "If Mama's finished the mending, bring my pullover shirt to Sonny's."

Sonny's? I can't believe it. I thought he'd wised up about Sonny. Every time I start to think Ben's gonna straighten up and fly right, he pulls something stupid like going back to the No-Nos. I think Mama got it wrong when she called Ben "strong." He's not strong, he's stubborn and foolish, just like Papa said. If he wants his shirt so bad, he can come and get it himself. I say good-bye to Tom and rejoin my friends. On the way out, I toss Ben's note in the trash barrel.

11

Taking It Too Far

忠義

The mess hall will be busting with people tonight, mostly young folks and kids from all over camp and maybe a few older people, too, from our block. When I get there, Tom and the others have already pushed the tables to the edges of the room to make room for the dancers, and they've waxed the floor. I help the Downbeats carry in their band instruments and chairs and then help Miss McAllister arrange a table in the corner where she can sell war savings stamps to the kids for their bond books. For my help, she buys me a 10-cent stamp for my own book. I tuck it deep into my pocket.

After that, I mostly sit back and watch Kiomi and some of the other girls from our block string a few streamers from the rafters.

"I like the streamers," I say.

"I wish we had more, but this is all we could get."

Kiomi frowns.

"But it still looks good."

She puts her hands on her hips and cocks her head.

"It does. Really!" I insist.

"Thanks, Tai." She brushes my arm with her hand.

"Would you like to dance later?" I ask.

"I'd love to. Come and find me when the music starts."

I say I will and then make like I have to help Tom take tickets at the door. He stands on one side of the doorway, and I stand on the other. The kids are streaming in, the guys in jackets and pullover sweaters and the girls in skirts and blouses. Everyone is talking excitedly and the temperature is rising, even with the door open.

Shig and Buck arrive with some of the other guys, and they try to lure me away from my post. I tell them to wait for me in the northeast corner, and I'll be there as soon as I can. The music starts right on time, and there's a rush of excitement as people try to push past each other to get in the door. One of the girls squeals so loud, she makes my ear ring. Tom laughs at me as I wiggle my ear as if trying to shake out the sound. I laugh too, until I hear that voice.

"What's the joke?" Sonny says.

He's standing there with his sunglasses on, though it's evening now.

"Nothin'" I say, looking at my shoes.

"Where's your brother?"

"Isn't he with you?" I ask.

"Nope. Haven't seen him all day."

"Maybe he's finishing up work."

"Nah, I got him to quit that job days ago."

I look up now. "What do you mean?"

"Is that what you want your brother doin', Tai? Cleaning the *hakujin's* toilets?"

"They're *our* toilets, Sonny," Tom says. "Someone's gotta clean them. Sure as heck's not gonna be you."

Sonny turns on Tom. "Rumor has it you've signed up for the draft, Tom. Wanna go fight in the white man's army, huh?"

"That's right," Tom says. "Some of us aren't afraid to fight."

Sonny puffs out his chest and inches up close to Tom. He tips his head back so he can scrutinize Tom from under his aviator glasses. "You callin' me a coward?"

Tom steps up to meet Sonny, so they're standing chest to chest. Some of the people nearby turn to watch.

"Back off, Tom," I hear my brother say. He pushes past the goons who've come with Sonny and moves in between Sonny and Tom.

"Come on, Sonny," Ben says with a slight glance in my direction. "We don't want trouble."

"Sure we do, Benjiro," Sonny says. "That's exactly what we want."

"Not here," Ben says. "There's too many people. Let's just go."

"Yeah, okay," Sonny says. "There's nothin' but kids here anyway." He turns to survey the room. With those sunglasses on, it's hard to see exactly where he's looking, but I think for a moment that his gaze pauses on the door at the opposite side of the barracks, the one behind the band. It's propped open to let the air in. There's no one standing there taking tickets. A slight smile crosses his lips. Maybe Sonny plans to sneak in that way. He turns and claps a hand on Ben's shoulder, and the two of them step outside.

I follow as far as the doorway and watch them go, Sonny still with his hand on Ben's shoulder, his goons following along behind. I watch till they round the corner of the barracks then excuse myself and dash to the opposite door. I peek out, but no one is there except some seagulls picking at the trash in the barrel. I stay there for several minutes standing guard, feeling pretty big on myself till I realize I have no idea what I'll do if Sonny does come back, especially if he comes without Ben. But after ten minutes, I'm bored, and the Downbeats are playing a swing song. The kids are all doing the Lindy Hop, trying out their "jigwalks" and "Suzy-Qs." I'm not much of a jive bomber myself, but I look around for Kiomi, wondering if I should ask her to dance anyway, but I don't see her.

I maneuver around the crowded room until I find Shig and Buck in the northeast corner, where I told them to wait. They've been joined by several other boys our age, and they're all talking about the basketball game that afternoon. Our team won, of course, but Shig came down sideways on a jump and twisted his ankle. He's retelling the story as if we hadn't all been there to see it. It's just plain hot in the mess hall now, with all the people crowded in. The music is loud enough it makes it difficult to talk, so mostly we just watch the dancers and point to girls we think one of us should ask to dance, including Kiomi. But none of us moves toward them. When the Downbeats announce they're taking a break, the whole room sighs with disappointment. Buck nudges me and says, "Come on, I need to go to the latrine."

"Well, you don't need my help."

"Just come on."

I toss a few words at Shig to let him know where we're heading then follow Buck out the main door. We hurry to the latrine, but we don't run. Only little kids run to the bathroom. Still, I want to get back as soon as I can. We don't get the Downbeats at our block dances very often. They're too busy playing everywhere else in camp.

When Buck finishes, we do run back. I realize the back door is probably closer, so I pull Buck down the street that runs along the back side of the mess hall. As we come up closer, though, I reach out an arm to stop him.

"What's that?" I say.

"What?"

"Those guys by the trash barrel. What're they doin'?"

Buck leans forward. It's hard to see because it's dark, and the men have their backs to us. I get a strange feeling in my stomach and pull Buck around the side of the barracks so we can peek out.

"What's the big deal?" Buck says. "Looks like they're just diggin' in the trash."

"But why?"

"How would I know?"

Just then, one of the men turns slightly to his right. "That's Sonny," I say. "Come on!"

"Hold on," Buck says.

"But I have to see what he's doing." Just then it all becomes clear. Smoke is rising from a pile of crates next to the trash barrel. Sonny picks up a small crate that's on fire and slides it inside the doorway. He uses a stick to push it to the right of the door, which would put it just behind the stage. No one will notice it there until it's burning good and strong. Sonny and his goon are laughing about the smoke and panic it will cause. But if the wind picks up as it comes through the door, it could spread the sparks to the cloth backdrop behind the stage. I start to run, but Buck pulls me back.

"We don't wanna mess with Sonny," he says.

"But we have to do something."

"We'll go back in the front then. We'll tell somebody."

"That might be too late," I say. Just then I see my brother coming up at a run from the opposite direction. The way he's moving, he must have seen what Sonny did. When I see my brother, I know I have to help. I shake off Buck's hand and rush toward them. I glance over my shoulder, but Buck's not following.

I don't think my brother's seen me. His whole attention seems fixed on Sonny. He grabs him by the shirt with both hands and shoves him back against the barracks. "What're you doin'?" he demands. "My brother's in there."

"No I'm not, Ben, I'm here," I say.

He takes his eyes off of Sonny to look at me, and that's a mistake. Sonny punches him in the gut.

"Get off of me," Sonny says. "I need to get out of here."

"Why?" I say, coming up beside Ben. "So you can keep yourself out of trouble as always? Who you gonna blame this time? Ben? Yoshi?"

"You shut up!" Sonny shouts.

"Leave my brother alone," Ben says, straightening up, one arm still wrapped around his stomach.

"See, Ben, this is what he's like. Is this the kind of friend you want? Someone who leaves you high and dry? Someone who sets fires to buildings?"

"Let's go," Sonny says to his goon, but just then, Tom jumps out the back door with Buck right behind him. Tom blocks Sonny's path.

"You're not goin' anywhere," he says. "The MPs are on their way."

"Oh come on, Tom," Sonny says. "They've put the fire out already. No harm done." He tries to sidestep Tom, but Tom moves with him.

"Outta my way, Tom, unless you wanna get hurt."

"Where you going to go, Sonny? Where you going to hide in camp? You can't lie your way out of this one. We've got witnesses."

Sonny keeps his eyes on Tom, but he reaches for one of his goons. "Give me the knife," he says. It's just like Sonny to make someone else carry his weapon.

The goon hands Sonny a knife made from a sharpened piece of metal tied with string to a wooden handle, and we all step back.

Sonny brandishes the knife in front of him. "Still itchin' for a fight, Tom? I'll give you one," he says. He laughs as Tom retreats. "Yeah, who's the coward now?" Sonny says. Then he turns to my brother. "Benjiro, when the MPs come, don't tell them it was me. Tell them it was someone else. Your brother's the only one who saw it. It'll be your word against a kid's."

I can feel Ben's eyes on me. I try to meet his gaze, but I'm afraid of what I'll see in his face. I'm afraid he'll let me down again, even after this.

"Forget it, Sonny," Ben says. "I'm not turnin' on my brother for you. Not this time."

"Yeah, and I saw it too," Buck says, coming up beside me. Shig and some of the other kids are gathered in the doorway now, watching, and the audience seems to make Sonny nervous. He opens and shuts his hand around the knife, and beads of sweat trickle down either side of his face. He jabs the knife at Tom to keep him back, but he doesn't try too hard to touch him. Without his sunglasses, Sonny looks much less cocky, and when the MPs with their rifles round the corner, he looks just plain scared. Tom springs forward and snatches the knife from Sonny. He sticks the knife into the waistband of his trousers and untucks his shirt to hide it.

The MPs look from one of us to the other, trying to figure out whom to arrest. Tom points at Sonny. "He's the one," Tom says.

"It's true," I say, a little too loud. "I saw him do it. And that one too." I point at the goon behind Sonny, and the MPs grab them both.

Sonny turns his meanest sneer on me, but it doesn't scare me anymore. I've seen what hides behind it. The MPs glance from me to Ben to Tom to Buck.

"One of you needs to come with us," an MP says. "Tell us what happened."

"I will," Ben offers.

"Ben, don't."

"It's okay, Tai. Tell Papa I'll see you at home tonight." He's standing straighter now, though still rubbing his sore stomach, and he gives me one of his slow smiles. He nods to the MPs and follows as they lead Sonny and his goon away.

When they're far enough away, I turn on Tom. "Why'd you hide the knife, Tom? Why'd you protect Sonny?"

"Sonny's a hothead, Tai, that's all. Setting a little fire is bad enough. No sense in them finding out he pulled a knife too. No telling what they'd do to him for that. Besides, things are bad enough around here without the guards thinking we've all got weapons." He turns to the group of kids who've gathered in the doorway. "Let's get back inside," he says. "You too, Tai."

I shake my head. "No, I'm going with my brother this time. He might need me. Will you tell my father, Tom?"

Tom nods. He puts both arms out and herds the rest of the kids back into the mess hall like a flock of complaining geese.

"Should I come too?" Buck says. "Or do you want me to stay here and keep an eye on Kiomi for ya?"

I shake my head. "You can stay."

"Thanks, buddy." Buck dashes back inside.

Shig is still standing beside me though. "That was cool what you did, standing up to Sonny."

"I didn't really. Ben did."

"You did too."

"You think Ben's gonna be okay? I don't mean now, Shig. I mean when my family leaves?"

"Yeah, he'll be fine," Shig says. "He's not with Sonny anymore. And he's safer here than in the war. Yoshi says if they do let us Japanese fight, they'll put us right up front where the fighting's worse. Maybe it was a good thing he signed no-no."

"That's true," I say, wondering why I never thought of it that way before.

"You better go if you're gonna catch up," Shig says.

"Do me a favor," I say, as I trot backwards facing Shig. "Keep Buck away from Kiomi. She's too good for him."

Shig laughs and disappears inside.

12

The Tournament

忠義

A few months later, on a hot August day, Papa and I wait by the bus to say good-bye to Tom. He's leaving for army basic training. Dan Hirata is shipping out too. Mama is standing by Dan's mother, holding baby Eiko, who is sleeping in Mama's arms. Mr. and Mrs. Hirata will be taking care of the baby while Dan is gone. None of us expected Dan to join the army, but he says the camp is too sad without Eiko, and he wants to do his part for the war effort. I watch as Mama lifts the baby to her cheek and nuzzles her. I can't tell for sure, but I think there are tears in her eyes.

Tom leaves his own family and comes over to Papa and me.

"Take care of yourself, Tom," Papa says, extending his hand.

"I will. You gonna let Tai take my place on the paper?"

"Perhaps," Papa says with a smile. "If he keeps up on his schooling."

Papa puts his hands behind his back and rocks up slightly on his toes. This is what he does when he's not sure what to say. Finally, he bows to Tom and inches closer to Mama.

I reach into my back pocket and take out the baseball card Eiko gave me. I've carried it with me all these weeks since she died. I straighten one of its bent corners as I glance at Dan, who's now holding his sleeping daughter, and wonder if Eiko would mind what I'm about to do. I decide she wouldn't, and I hold out the card.

"What's this?" Tom asks.

"It's a Lou Gehrig card."

"I thought you told me you left your collection behind."

"I did. Eiko gave this to me. I haven't shown it to anyone since she died. I want you to have it."

"I can't take it, Tai."

"I want you to."

"But it's your only card."

"That's just it. What's the point of one card without the whole collection?"

Tom studies the card for a moment.

"You sure?"

"Yeah, it can be your good luck charm."

"Tell you what, I'll give it back to you when I'm home from the war, okay?" Tom squeezes my shoulder like he always does, and I think how lonely it's going to be at the newspaper office without him.

Then a look of surprise crosses Tom's face. I follow his gaze and see Ben coming toward us, his hands tucked in the back pockets of his jeans, his head down as a gust of wind stirs up the dust.

"Hey ya, Ben," Tom says.

"Hey," Ben's head is still lowered.

"Like your new job at the mess hall?"

"Beats swabbin' toilets. Thanks for helping me get it."

"My brother told me about it," Tom said. "I just passed on the word."

"Well, thanks anyway."

When the bus driver calls for the men to board, my stomach flips. It feels all wrong for Tom to be leaving. What if Shig's right? What if they put him right up front in the fighting? I may never see him again. Tears sting the back of my eyes.

"Hey, do me a favor," Tom says, his voice choking. "Don't let this place get you down okay? You got that judo tournament in a few days, right? I expect you to win just like you said you would."

I straighten up and meet his gaze. "Okay, Tom," I say. "So go on then. Go get some Nazis."

He chucks me on the shoulder, rushes back to get his suitcase, and kisses his mother good-bye. Ben and I sidle a little closer to our parents. Mama smiles at Ben as he shakes Dan's hand. Mrs. Hirata cries as her son boards the bus. Dan takes a window seat, but Tom sits on the other side of the bus, where he can see his own family. Mama holds up baby Eiko, so Dan can see her better. He waves as the bus pulls away, and we wave back. When the dust settles, I see Tom's family huddled together. They nod to us, and we nod to them. We have something in common now more than just friendship. We have *Nisei* soldiers in the war.

Mama hands the baby back to Mrs. Hirata, who's still crying softly.

"I'm glad you came, Benjiro," Mama says, squeezing my brother's hand. "We're going to the Hiratas. Would you like to come, Tai?"

I know she wants me to, but I picture Eiko's apartment with both Eiko and Dan now gone and Mrs. Hirata still upset, and I shake my head.

Mama nods her understanding. She turns her attention back to Ben. "You are thin," she says. "Are you eating enough?"

"Yes, Mama."

"Hmm," she says. She squeezes his hand again and smiles at me over her shoulder as she goes to join Papa and the Hiratas.

"I'm headin' to the rec hall to play ping-pong with the guys," I say to Ben. "Wanna come?"

"Why not? I got nothin' else to do."

We start the long walk back to our block. At first neither of us speaks, then the silence gets to me.

"I wonder what it's like," I say.

"What?"

"Going off to war."

Ben says nothing.

"Do you think they're scared?"

"I don't know about Tom, but Dan is."

"How do you know?"

"He told me. He's afraid if he dies over there, things will be hard on his baby. His parents are older, you know?"

"Mama will help," I say.

"Yeah, if we all stay together." Ben stops. "I mean if *you* all stay together."

"You'll be with us too, Ben. After the war. We'll all be together then."

"I guess."

We walk a few more paces in silence.

"Do you wish you were going too?" I ask.

"Do you mean do I wish I hadn't signed no-no? No, it was the right thing to do. I hate this camp, Tai. I hate what the government did to us."

I know he means it, but I'm glad there's not as much anger in his voice anymore when he says it. I risk a glance at my brother, but he's watching his feet. I can't say for sure if Ben is still mixed up with the No-No Boys, but at least he's not with Sonny. Sonny was arrested and taken to the jail in the nearby town. They sent him there not just because he started the fire, but because he had refused to sign the questionnaire altogether. We're not sure how long they'll keep him or any of the others they've rounded up, but I hope it's for a while. Without Sonny around, Ben has a better chance of staying out of trouble.

When we get to the rec hall, Kiomi is standing outside with a couple of her friends. She signals for me to wait.

Ben nudges me. "Looks like your girlfriend wants

ya."

"She's not my girlfriend."

Ben laughs. He takes his time walking up the couple of steps into the recreation hall, and Kiomi waits until he's inside to say, "I need to tell you something, Tai."

"What?"

"My dad wrote to a Caucasian man he knows who owns a farm in Utah. Papa asked him to sponsor us to come work on his farm. If his friend says yes, we could be leaving the camps."

"That's great, Kiomi."

"Would you maybe write to me, Tai?"

"Do you want me to?"

She frowns. "Only if you want to."

"I don't know. I'm not even sure where I'm gonna wind up."

"Well, I could give you my address, and then you could write no matter where you are."

I hear Buck and Shig snickering inside, and something tells me it's about me. "Let's just wait and see if you go," I say to Kiomi. "No sense talkin' 'bout something that hasn't happened yet."

"Fine," she says.

"Kiomi, wait."

When she turns back to me, I can't think of anything to say. Then my eyes light on her necklace, made of tiny white seashells. "Um, did you make that?"

"Yes."

"It's pretty."

She fingers the necklace and smiles. "Thanks, Tai."

"Come on, Kiomi," her friend calls. As I watch her go, I recall the latest rumors in camp. They say the government will be moving those of us who signed yes-yes to other camps soon. Buck's dad heard that they might not make all yes-yes families leave, though. If they don't, his dad says they'll stay in Tule Lake, even though some people will assume they're disloyal because they stayed. Shig's family will stay too because they signed no-no. And so will Ben. But my father is still determined to leave, which means I'll be going too.

When we first came to Tule Lake, I knew things weren't great, but at least we were together. Now I wonder if I'll know anyone in the new camp, if there will be any boys there from our old neighborhood. And I wonder which camp they'll send us to, and if it will be different from Tule Lake or the same. I wonder how long we'll have to stay there before we can go home to Japantown. Before we can be a family again.

But then I remember my promise to Tom about keeping my chin up, and I hurry into the rec hall before my thoughts can get to me. Ben is concentrating on bouncing the ping-pong ball up and down on the paddle. Buck is laughing as he tries to wrestle the other paddle away from Shig.

"Tai, help me."

"No fair," Shig yelps as I lunge for the paddle. Now Ben is laughing too.

Even with the windows open, it's blistering hot in the high school auditorium today. My judo uniform is heavy with my perspiration, and I swipe my sleeve across my forehead to keep the sweat out of my eyes. But I'm trying not to think about any of that as I wait at the outside edge of our mat for Sensei to call Shig and me forward. Shig is waiting on the opposite edge. We've each been winning all day against other opponents. Now we face each other in the final match. The tournament will be won or lost in this round, but I try not to think of that, either. When you're focused on winning, Sensei says, your whole body becomes too tense. You can't move as freely as you need to. So I tell myself it doesn't matter if I win, and I try to keep my muscles loose.

When Sensei finally calls us forward, I can't feel the heat in the room anymore. All I feel is an awful fluttering in my stomach and my eyebrows knitting together as I lock eyes with Shig. We step up to our lines and bow to each other. Then I stand inside my line, with my hands to my sides and my feet apart. There's a hint of a smile on Shig's face. He knows he's going to win. I feel my eyes narrow even more, and I tell myself to stay loose. The audience is growing restless in the heat. The men are fanning themselves with their hats, the women with their judo programs. At the exact moment Sensei says *hajime*, "begin," I hear Ben yell, "*Gambatte*!" My father yells it too. Several men do. And my heart picks up its pace.

I reach for Shig, and we grab hold of each other. I try to sense his moves before he makes them. I can feel his muscles tense, and I know he's going to throw me. He turns his back and bends his knees, but I recognize this throw, and I swing my body to my left as I fall. I land on my side, not my back, so Shig doesn't get the full point, but he drops down and immediately pins me. He's even stronger than usual today. He wants to win. I'm breathing strenuously as I struggle to squeeze out from under him. I know the time keeper is counting, and if he makes it to twenty-five seconds, Shig will win the match. I turn to my right and then my left, but Shig isn't budging. Finally, I plant my feet and arch my back and push against him with all my strength. To my surprise, his weight shifts over my head and his hold breaks.

I struggle to my feet. I'm tired now, but so is Shig. We grab onto each other, each trying to move into position for a throw. Shig leans forward and, without thinking, I move into *harai goshi*. I haven't tried this throw since the night Shig and I argued over his father's loyalty. I threw him easily then, but he'd been distracted by his father's decision. Surely I can't do it again.

I step to the right and bring my leg back across his. As I feel his feet come off the ground and his weight shift over my hip, I know I've done it. He's falling, and I'm struggling to keep upright myself. When he hits the mat, I hear my brother cheer. I glance up to see Ben leap to his feet, waving his hat. My father stands too, clapping proudly. My mother stays seated, but she smiles at me warmly. The whole match took less than a minute and a half, but it felt so much longer. I breathe in deeply and feel my chest swell. Sensei awards me *ippon*, a full point. We bow to each other, and the match is over. I've won!

Shig stands, both hands on his lower back. "Well, you got me," he says. "It was the heat, you know? Makes you tired."

"Yeah, sure," I say, not wanting to rub things in. "I thought you had me earlier with that pin."

"But I couldn't hang on."

"Must have been the heat," I taunt. Shig glares at me, then we both laugh.

Across the auditorium, our friends and families are waiting at the edge of the mats. Ben is here, and Buck and Jimi and the guys, and Kiomi and her friends. As happy as I am to see them, I wish Tom were here, and Dan and Eiko. When I think of them, I feel a twinge of sadness. Then I remember what my father told me a few days ago. One of the horrible windstorms had just blown through camp, coating everything with thick dust. "I hate this stupid camp," I'd yelled.

"*Gaman*, Taichirou," Papa had said. "Patience. One day this war will end."

He's right, of course. One day this war will end. And when it does, Tule Lake will be just a memory. And what I think I'll remember most is this tournament and playing basketball with my friends and that day on the mountain when my mother showed me it's not what's done to us that counts, but how we endure it. *Shikata ga nai.*

Meet the Real Kids of Tule Lake

Mas Yamasaki, George Nakano and Mary Kawano Fong

Tai's story is mostly made up, as any good piece of fiction is. But in many ways, Tai's story started with my high school P.E. teacher, George Nakano, who told us snippets about growing up in a Japanese internment camp during WWII. Since I was not very athletic, Mr. Nakano would have had no reason to remember me, but I always remembered him. And when it came time to write *The No-No Boys*, I called him. Like Tai's parents, Mr. Nakano's mother was a picture bride who came from Japan to America to marry his father, whom she'd never met. And like Tai, Mr. Nakano was a kid who loved sports. Mr. Nakano had a younger sister who died in the camp, which led me to include the death of Tai's beloved cousin, Eiko, and Mr. Nakano's memories of hearing about Pearl Harbor are the same as Tai's. Mr. Nakano was never held at Tule Lake. His family was sent to Poston Camp in Arizona, where I imagine Tai went after he left Tule Lake.

But this story also belongs to a wonderful man named Masaru Yamasaki. Mas shared with me many details of the teenage years he spent at Tule Lake. Like Tai, Mas's parents had owned a tofu shop in Japantown in Sacramento. And like Tai, Mas loved basketball and football and hanging out with his friends. Mas had also participated in judo before the war, but like Tai, his father burned his uniform after the war started. And Mas had a collection of baseball cards he was forced to leave behind, along with everything else he cared about, including his hard-won bag of marbles. Mas's father signed no-no on the questionnaire for the same reason Shig's father does in my story, not because he was disloyal, but because he wanted to keep his family in California. But Mas, like a lot of kids whose families had signed no-no, was bothered his whole life by the realization that some people would always think of him as disloyal because of what his father felt forced to do.

Mary Kawano Fong has been troubled by something different. Her father signed yes-yes on the questionnaire, but like Buck's family, the Fongs decided to stay at Tule Lake. For years after the war, many people thought that meant her family had chosen to be disloyal. To this day, some people still believe that. During the war, Mary's older sister wanted to give up her American citizenship, so she could marry a young man whose family planned to move back to Japan. Mary's father wouldn't allow it. "You were lucky to be born here," her father said. "You would be crazy to stop being an American." I'd known all along that I wanted Ben to feel differently than his father about the question of loyalty, and the story of Mary's sister helped me realize how difficult those disagreements must have been on families.

Japanese parents tended to be pretty strict, and back then kids didn't get to express their opinions as they do today. The real-life Japanese-Americans I interviewed for this book told me they respected the decisions their fathers and older brothers made, even though all of those decisions were different. They learned from that experience that just because someone believes something different than you, he's not necessarily wrong.

So what happened to these former Tule Lake kids? Well, you already know that the athletic boy named George grew up to be my P.E. teacher. Ironically, Mas also considered teaching P.E., but he was discouraged from trying, since in those days, not many people would hire a Japanese-American teacher. So Mas went into business instead. And Mary worked as a clerk for the State of California's Education Department. When they reminisce about the camps now, all three mention the hardships and injustices, but they also remember fondly the good friends they made, the fun they had and the respect and love they felt for their families. As Mary says, "I just did the best I could to get along, enjoy it, laugh, be happy, because that's what my father told me to do."

By the way, the illustration of the boy on the cover is Mas!

If You'd Been Friends with Tai Shimoda

If you'd been friends with Tai Shimoda, you might have:

Built several COLLECTIONS. Like children of all eras, the kids of World War II loved to collect things: comic books, marbles, stamps, coins, paper dolls, toy soldiers, bottle caps, movie magazines, dolls, etc. But one of the most popular collections for boys, of course, was baseball cards. Baseball cards have been around since the 1800s. Tai's cards would probably have come from the Goudey Gum Company issue. They had hand-colored pictures of players on the front and biographical information on the back. Tai and his cousin, Eiko, would have gotten them in packs of gum or traded to get them from friends. As with many things, production of baseball cards slowed down during World War II, due partly to shortages of paper and ink. After the war, baseball card production picked up again. If you'd been friends with Tai, it's very likely you would have had to leave most of your collections behind when you went to the camps, but some kids did keep one or two of their favorite items.

Enjoyed listening to MUSIC. In the days before television, music and dancing were primary sources of entertainment. Big Band music was all the rage in the early 1940s. Band leaders like Glenn Miller, Benny Goodman and Tommy Dorsey played swing music (like the Downbeats in my story played), which got everyone dancing the foxtrot or Lindy Hop. Jazz musicians with colorful names like Cab Calloway, Dizzy Gillespie and Count Basie also influenced the music of the era. Many popular World War II songs were patriotic. Some, like "Boogie Woogie Bugle Boy," were inspired by army life. Many others, like "I'll Be Seeing You," spoke to the sadness of missing a soldier overseas or a girl back home. Songs like "White Cliffs of Dover" or "As Time Goes By" were played over and over, and to this day bring back memories of World War II to anyone who lived then.

Followed the exploits of the 442nd. The 442nd Regimental Combat Team was made up of Japanese-American soldiers, many of whom came from or had family members in the camps. The unit's motto was "Go for Broke," which meant they'd be willing to risk everything to win. And so they did! They battled the Germans in Italy, France and Germany. They fought hard and well, partly to prove to their fellow countrymen that they were loyal Americans. No other unit in U.S. history has been as decorated as the 442nd. Because they'd won so many medals, they were called "The Purple Heart Battalion." Boys Tai's age tracked the movements of the 442nd with great pride.

STARTED OVER after the war. Like Tai's family, many of the Japanese sent to the camps lost everything in the evacuation. After the war, some of them returned to their former towns to start over. Others took advantage of offers from friends to relocate to new places. Some of the young men found it hard to find work because people preferred to give jobs to returning soldiers—but also because many Americans still didn't trust the Japanese. In many towns after the war, it was not uncommon to find signs on shops, restaurants and other public places that said "No Japs Allowed." Despite the difficulties and the prejudice, Japanese-Americans worked diligently, proved themselves on the job and slowly rebuilt their lives. Boys Tai's age would have returned to high school when the war ended. In most cases, they were glad to be back amongst old friends.

Glossary

Arigato gozaimasu – thank you very much

Baishakunin – matchmaker

Baka! – stupid

Caucasian – English word for white people

Deru kui wa utareru – "the stake that sticks out gets hammered down"

Gaman – be patient

Gambatte – do your best, fight well

Go – a popular Japanese board game

Hajime – begin

Hakujin – white person

Hana – a Japanese card game

Harai goshi – a judo throw

Inu – a spy or informer

Issei – people born in Japan who moved to America, first-generation immigrants

Jap – a common but unkind word during World War II to describe people of Japanese ancestry

Loyals – those who signed yes-yes on the loyalty questionnaire

Kimono – a traditional Japanese garment

Ne-waza – groundwork in judo

Nisei – the children of Issei, second generation born in the U.S.

No-Nos – those who signed no-no on the loyalty questionnaire

Osaewaza – pinning techniques

Reigi – proper etiquette

Samurai – Japanese warriors of the upper class

Sensei – teacher or master

Shikata ga nai – "it can't be helped"

Tofu – a popular food in the Japanese diet made of soybean curds

Questions 27 and 28 of the War Department's and War Relocation Authority's Loyalty Questionnaire, which helped separate the Loyals from the Disloyals (also called No-Nos):

No. 27. Are you willing to serve in the armed forces of the United States on combat duty wherever ordered?

No. 28. Will you swear unqualified allegiance to the United States of America and faithfully defend the United States from any or all attack by foreign or domestic forces, and forswear any form of allegiance or obedience to the Japanese emperor, to any other foreign government, power or organization?

Acknowledgments

One of the things I like best about being a writer is talking to people who know a lot about subjects I know nothing about. I get to learn new things every day, so I never get bored! Virgil Leenerts and Larry Olson know a lot about radios, and they helped me figure out how Tai could build a shortwave in camp. My brother, Mike Rupp, knows a lot about judo. He's a black belt, and he helped me write the judo scenes in this book. I thank them for sharing their time and expertise with me!

And, of course, I got to learn all about growing up in Japanese internment camps from three very special people. You will learn more about my new friends in the Meet the Real Kids of Tule Lake section in the back of this book. But there was one other person who helped me understand and appreciate what life would have been like for Tai. His name is Jimi Yamaichi, and he lived at Tule Lake as a grown-up. Jimi's an expert on the camp, and he shared details I couldn't find anywhere else. Thank you, Jimi!

Every day, my publishing partner, Karla Oceanak, and I uncover something new about how to write and produce good books. Karla shares her knowledge with me and her tremendous talent, and she helps make my books better in every way. I don't know anything about being an artist or a designer, so I'm always excited to see how Kendra Spanjer and Launie Parry will take our simple suggestions and turn them into amazing book covers. To all the amazing women at Linden, thank you! And to my long-time writer friends and members, past and present, of the Slow Sand Writers Society and SCBWI and CIPA organizations, a special thanks for passing on your learning to me.

My biggest teachers, though, are my kids, who read the early drafts of my stories and offer suggestions. My son, Brian, is the same age as Tai, and I confess I looked at him for a model in some ways. My daughter, Lydia, is a careful and insightful reader and gives me great feedback. And my youngest daughter, Ava, is such a strong supporter of my work that she once set up a table to sell my books at the end of our driveway. I'm lucky to have such helpful, encouraging kids!

And I'm especially lucky to have a husband who likes to learn along with me. He's helped me in so many ways I can't list them all here. But he knows. And he knows I couldn't do it without him. That's why this book is dedicated to him.

About the Author

Teresa R. Funke writes for children and adults. Most of her books and short stories are based on real people and actual events, and many are set in World War II. She says, "I chose the *The No-No Boys* for my second book in the Home-Front Heroes collection because when I first started learning about World War II as a child, I thought America had done everything right. Then I found out there was this one thing we'd done terribly wrong. Like the schoolchildren I speak to today, I felt a little let down, but I also felt inspired by the Japanese-Americans who, despite everything, never stopped believing in this country. Because of people like them, I've never stopped believing, either!"

Teresa also enjoys teaching new writers as a popular presenter and writers' coach, but what she likes best is spending time with her husband and three children at their home in Colorado. She'd love it if you visited her website at **www.teresafunke.com** to submit your own family's stories from World War II or other time periods, or to invite Teresa to speak at your school.

Coming Soon From Teresa R. Funke

The Newest Home-Front Hero

Twelve-year-old Miguel Montoya has been left behind. His brothers have joined the service during World War II, and his sisters are working to support the war effort. Miguel is expected to take their places in the family grocery store. But living in San Antonio, Texas—one of the most exciting military cities in the country—Miguel would rather be helping win the war than stocking shelves. So when Miguel is also asked to watch his troublesome little nephew, he rebels. But then the realities of war hit home, and it is Miguel who must hold the family together and save his nephew from danger.